Morrigan's Shadows

This book is dedicated to my family, including loved ones who are like family. Without your encouragement, I would have defeated myself a long time ago. Thank you all for everything.

Copyright © 2012 Michelle Barclay
All rights reserved. This book
may not be reproduced, transmitted or distributed in whole or in part
without the express written permission of the copyright holder, except
as applies to fair rights use.

Printed in the United States of America

First Printing, 2012

ISBN 978-1477545720

Chapter 1

The room was warm enough to make her skin moist. Morrigan Fuseli removed her sweatshirt and draped it over the arm of the leather couch upon which she was seated, waiting for Dr. Bateson to occupy the seat directly across from her.

The office she waited in was one with which she was quite familiar, having spent at least one hour per week in it for the past year. All of the psych books, mythology books and correlating statuettes that filled the bookshelves in the room had once drawn her attention, but now there was nothing of interest, save the imposing man who had been her sole sounding board for the anxiety, night terrors and insomnia that had plagued her for so long.

Dr. Bateson settled his expansive frame in the equally expansive chair across from Morrigan and spared a brief, but sincere smile for her.

"Ms. Fuseli. How are things?"

She hated being referred to as Ms. Fuseli. It was not petulance that made her feel this way so much as a sense that a stranger was being addressed, but that she had to answer. No one but Dr. Bateson called her Ms. Fuseli, but she never bothered to correct him.

"Its life, big guy. Not much has changed since last week. How's your life?"

They made small talk like this for half an hour before Morrigan broke the bubble that surrounded her outside Bateson's office and started talking about the things that really bothered her.

"You look tired, Morrigan." It usually took Bateson a few minutes to lapse into a first name conversation, no matter how many times they saw each other.

"I actually slept pretty well last night. I had a monster of an anxiety attack this morning, though. I thought I was going to wind up canceling with you and putting another chef on for tonight." They both knew she would have done neither in any situation where she retained consciousness. Morrigan always adhered to her schedule. By saying she would have deviated, she was expressing the severity of her attack.

"What about the rest of the week?"

"Nightmares every night that I slept and during my impromptu naps, save one. However, there was only one other anxiety attack, that I can remember."

"So no change in frequency and severity of either?" He always asked the same question. He also always got the same answer.

"Nothing that I can notice."

He lifted his shaggy red-bearded face from the notebook in his lap and looked Morrigan in the eye. Another common question was coming.

"Have you given medication any more thought?"

"I have and I am still not interested." Morrigan hated feeling anything but fully herself, hence her hatred of the anxiety. She had had vivid nightmares and insomnia for most of her adult life and occasionally during her childhood, but the first time she got whacked with an anxiety attack, she scheduled an appointment with Dr. Bateson before the symptoms had dissipated. At that initial appointment and ever since, she had been refusing to take medication.

The first time she met Dr. Bateson, Morrigan was surprised. She had been expecting a diminutive man with a high-pitched voice, bifocals and an annoying tweed suit. A bald spot came and went in her imaginings.

Morrigan Fuseli spent a lot of time envisioning precisely what would happen in every scenario in her life. She was typically close enough to give her a sense of pride in her intuition. It gave her an illusion of stability. She was dead wrong in Bateson's case. The man was more than six feet tall, barrel-chested and topped with a mass of red head and facial hair. He had a slight spattering of freckles across the bridge of his nose that almost led one to make the mistake of thinking he was mischievous. He wasn't. A more serious and somber man Morrigan had never met.

Dr. Bateson was very different from Morrigan in many ways. He was never one to imagine the outcome of any given day. He knew it was just added stress. While he was carefully reserved, he was also carefree. He did not obsess. He just took things as they happened. That did not stop him from being taken aback by Morrigan Fuseli the first time he saw her. Most people were.

She was a statuesque 5'10 with emerald green eyes, midnight black hair and she could only be described as breathtaking. She had been dressed quite casually in a gray knit sweater, jeans and Converse high tops, but there was no mistaking her beauty or the ease with which she came by it. Bateson admired her, but not as other men might. He merely locked the information that she was gorgeous away in his mind's cupboard and treated her like any other patient. He took things as they came, but he knew the time and place for everything and never varied.

"You have to get out of your comfort zone every now and then if you want these attacks to stop, Morrigan. The only help I can give you is behavioral, if it cannot be medicinal. Do something that makes you anxious and stick with it until the anxiety passes. I have told you before. We can do those things together until you feel better."

"I don't have time to do anything as non-specific as "get out of my comfort zone," doc. If you want me to pencil in dinner and a movie, I can handle that. It's predictable and I know how long it will take." She winked at him across the gap between them. She really did not expect the handsome beast of a man to date her nor she him, but she liked watching his response, as nondescript as it always was.

"No, thank you. How about I pick you up at a random time on your day off and we do something surprising of my choosing?"

"Not a chance in hell, doc. I know where we are going and how long it will take or it is a no go."

"Honestly, Morrigan. How do you run a restaurant in this town if you cannot stand the unpredictable?"

"Nothing in my kitchen is unpredictable. The chaos is quite organized." She smiled somewhat proudly at this.

"All right, then why do you come here? You have your parameters. You refuse to remove yourself from them. You will not take medication. You will not try behavioral therapy. Nothing about your conditions have changed since you started coming here. So, why?"

"Because I would feel crazy if I didn't."

He favored her with one of his rare laughs and tossed his notebook onto the table. "Time is up, Morrigan. I suppose I will see you next week."

She smiled, stood up, gave him a perfunctory wave and a genuine smile as she walked out into the afternoon sunshine.

Two hours later, in checks and a chef jacket, Morrigan stood in the walk-in counting beef cuts and wondering who to banish to salad land tonight. Every person on her five-man line could cook anything in the restaurant and every single one of them hated salads.

~~~~~~~~~~

Marking down the last number on her count, a shivering Morrigan emerged from the walk-in and shouted, "Shift meeting!" without looking up. At Morrigan's, her shift meeting consisted solely of back of the house staff. She hired very good people to deal with the scavengers at the front of the house so she rarely had to mingle with them.

She wandered out of the back door to the smoking area where she briefed her staff each afternoon. She looked up from her clipboard long enough to accept a lit cigarette from Monty -- her highest paid, if you tell any of the rest of them I will murder you, cook. From the corner of the mouth not wrapped around a Marlboro filter the word salad emerged and each cook cringed. She settled the clipboard on her lap and looked up. "I'll cut a deal with you babies. I will sling lettuce tonight, if," groans from every direction, "one of you picks up a pit shift for Angelo."

Mikey, the 20-year-old with two babies and a mortgage stepped forward and offered to take it. Morrigan would have to wiggle his already crammed schedule around, but accepted. "Nice. Let's get to the specials . . . "

It was a marathon, like any other Friday night. Morrigan covered salads, as promised, but she also became the back up for every station that went down that night and they all did more than once. She was running on a good night's sleep, though and her anxiety was long forgotten. She was in her element. She was a maestro and then, she was done for the night. Clean up, lock down, go home and do it again tomorrow. That was her life.

Morrigan had been the owner of Morrigan's for nearly five years. She opened the restaurant at the ripe old age of 19, with her business partner and best friend. Within the year, Cora moved to Italy with one of their line cooks, leaving Morrigan to buy out the other half of what was then Cora and Morrigan's. She was more than happy to do it. Cora, or at least her crotch, was a distraction to the male staff in the back of the house. Morrigan used to say, "You can take the kitchen out of the whore, get the whore out of my kitchen." Cora would laugh, but she eventually obliged – in love for what seemed like the hundredth time since they had met. That was that. Morrigan loved her kitchen and worried all the time that her mental would ruin this for her. So far, it only had her falling asleep in the walk-in, office and dry storage from time to time.

For reasons unknown to Morrigan Fuseli, stepping into a dark room was much like sinking in a warm bath on a cold winter night to others. There was something about the darkness that made her comfortable, like her thoughts did not drift off into nowhere, as if the shadows themselves were holding the chaos that she was so afraid of in check. In a way, it was as if she was the orchestrator of the darkness. She was writer of her own shadowy composition. The darkness was an abyss that she could color any way she wished.

As she stepped into her dark apartment that Thursday, she did what she always did -- she savored a moment of her shadowy fairy tale. She painted the abyss with darkscapes only she could understand. Like so many others, she imagined horrors in the recesses of darkness, but they were her horrors. They were not unfamiliar or frightening. They were more predictable than any other aspect of her life because she had spent more time painting the shades of shadows and darkness than she had spent doing anything else in her life. Her night terrors, her insomnia, they were both part of this aspect of Morrigan, a part of her she could never explain, though she never tried. Not even with the good doc. She flipped on the light.

There it was again. The harsh light of reality. Counter tops designed by others, furniture, comfortable, yet alien. Appliances she never would have worked into her world of shadows. They were familiar. Therefore, they were not frightening, but still, they were not comforting. She always imagined that was why she loved to make food. She was in control of the colors, the tastes the textures and even the temperatures.

Like her nightscapes, food was something that was enjoyed on an utterly personal level. No matter what recipe you follow, it was never exactly the same. No matter who you fed it to, it was experienced differently. She liked to affect people on a personal level, though she loathed having the shoe on the other foot. She wouldn't even let people cook for her or drive with her in a vehicle. She walked mostly everywhere and drove herself everywhere else. Her long dead parents had a hell of a time driving her in the car from the moment she left the hospital and entered the rest of the world for the first time.

She ate a meal that was nowhere near the quality of the authentic Greek cuisine she served at Morrigan's. She donned wool knit socks that stretched up to her slender knees, gym shorts and a long tank top, then plopped herself in front of her laptop, wondering if sleep would come tonight.

Morrigan finally drifted off at 7 in the morning after spending hours with the light off, painting the abyss with her nightscapes.

Chapter 2

Polished onyx.

That is the only comparison Morrigan's musing mind can make. Thin, many branched trees of polished onyx as far as she can see in any direction, which is not far. All dreams are limited this way. Like the sides of a snow globe, nightmarish landscapes in the sleeping world can only meander so far before poking at the edges of reality and recoiling from the prospect of spreading too far. The cold, hard edges of the globe remind the landscape that waking the dreamer trapped within will mean its demise, possibly forever. The trees huddle well within their boundaries.

Morrigan walks along, though she has no awareness of her feet, of exertion or any other such mundane detail that the waking world would contain. Every so often, her head snaps up. She is viewing the world through her eyes, so she does not see herself walking through the surreal forest. She can only tell that her head and feet are moving by the way her vision of the trees changes with the movement. As she adjusts her view to peer closer at the unnaturally beautiful trees, she sees a viscous, oily substance dripping from them. It hardens into their gleaming surfaces as she watches.

Craaack! They all move away from her, creating a semi-circle of shining, black floor. Their movement is synchronized, controlled and halted rapidly. It is then that she notices they are all the same tree. The moment the realization comes, they all disappear, save one. Beside it, stands the Winged Man. His head is slightly long, chiseled and painfully handsome. A mop of curly black hair adorns his head. His long neck sits atop broad shoulders that lead down to a tapering, broad chest. His arms look impossibly strong as he wraps them around the tree, squeezing, cracking its exterior, revealing a turquoise blue sap that drips like blood from the trees black bark.

The Winged Man is a familiar figure in Morrigan's dreams. His face has been part of her life longer than that of her parents. His unbelievable strength, powerful posture and unassuming presence have long made Morrigan's nightmaring self admire him. There is something new tonight, though, something almost sinister. To Morrigan, very little of what most would deem nightmares is sinister. She accepts nightmarish horror while discussing it with herself, a feat most people cannot accomplish while dreaming. Now she thinks, "What is different about him? What am I afraid of?"

The tree begins undulating against the Winged Man, as a black, sharp cornered house erects itself around the three of them -- Morrigan, the Winged Man and the tree. The tree's shape begins to shift. While it is changing, the man notices her looking at him and sneers at her, allowing his tongue to run over his beautiful, frightening lips. All the while the tree is changing into long-limbed woman with angelic features. She is wearing a turquoise blue gown that Morrigan can see the curve of her breasts and the shadow of her pubic region through. Her skin has transformed from ivory to alabaster, her arms lifted high above her head, the Winged Man's arms surrounding her waist as he stares at Morrigan.

The woman kisses the denizen of Morrigan's nightmares. Unable to reach his face with her lips, she caresses the skin of his arms and chest with her mouth. He looks bored with her, still looking slyly at Morrigan, who feels oddly ill at ease, as if something that has long been one way is changing. She steps back, intending to leave this source of her uneasiness and wander elsewhere until she wakes.

As she turns to go, the Winged Man gestures to Morrigan to come to him. His expression is one of pleading. She is confused and scared, but wanting to be with him in her strange, dark nightmares as she has done so many times before. She changes direction and takes several steps toward him, her eyes never leaving his hungry face. She is afraid, and yet . . .

Argh, light. The agony of instant exposure as her eyes open to another day. Even through the thick curtains, enough light inundates the room for Morrigan to see every alien detail of every item there. Gone are the odd angles, blending colors and black corners of her sleeping mind. What is this? She sits up, sweating and biting back a scream. Doc calls this moment and all those like it night terrors.

Morrigan knows that it is not so much the night or the content of her dreams that scare her. It is the waking. Waking into this whitewashed world. She becomes fully conscious and remembers that this is her life. This is where she must live. She doesn't cry as she would have a few years ago. She shuffles to her bathroom, strips off her clothes and showers in the dark.

Chapter 3

Four days after Morrigan's disturbing dream of the Winged Man, she is running on one night of sleep. Her infrequent naps at work have been dotted with the dark colors of her nightmares, but are never long enough to develop into anything interesting. Morrigan has thrown herself into work, as she usually does when sleep and dreams evade her.

She is walking to her restaurant when she sees a homeless man by the side of the road. He wears at least two pairs of pants, as evidenced by the color that pokes through the holes in the top pair. His shirt is an old flannel completely covered in pins that contain phrases like, "Jesus Saves," "Hell is for Sinners," and Morrigan's favorite, "The End is Nigh." It is clear that what was probably intended to be a gag pin is taken very seriously by the bedraggled man. He holds a sign that says, "2012 is not the end of the world. It is the end of your world. Repent now and be saved." It's February. Morrigan mentally remarks that 10 months of sporadic lunacy are ahead before another doomsday passes by uneventfully.

There is a coffee vendor not ten feet from the homeless doomsayer. Morrigan buys two mediums, pays and places one on the ground in front of the homeless man as she passes. It's a routine that both are used to, as is what comes next. "Buying coffee for homeless people won't save you!" he shouts after her, "You will be beheaded while I watch from paradise." Morrigan laughs to herself, but feels sympathetic. Poor bastard has to get his energetic fervor from somewhere.

The blonde, seriously endowed bartender Christine looks up from her prep as Morrigan walks in the door.

"Hey, Morrigan. It's going to be dead today and Janet looks like hell warmed over. Do you mind if I send her home and work the bar myself for lunch?"

"As long as you can swing it, we're good."

Morrigan knew she could swing it. Christine was exactly the type of bartender she loved. The kind of package every man fantasizes is a slut, but is actually a law student who hasn't been laid since she started law school a year ago. She never brings home customers, but makes them feel like she does it all the time. She giggles like a moron and then does all of Morrigan's bar numbers without ever messing them up.

"Christine, did you get Doomsey's muffin this morning?" Morrigan added, as she swung the door open to the kitchen.

Christine laughed, "Yeah, and I got a, 'Your tits won't save you, blondie' for my trouble."

"He really needs a new spiel. Maybe we should ask him what will save us some time."

"Pfft. I'm broke enough without shelling out what those wackos think of as salvation. I'll take my chances."

Tuesdays were dry shipment days. Morrigan hunted in huge piles of dry goods for bags of pasta, take out boxes and the like, while checking them off on her lists. Once the orders were signed for and counted, she began putting things in order. She always waited until the delivery guys were gone to put stuff away. She had the room for it, so she didn't bother with the chaos of rotating while the guys were traipsing in and out of the dock door. Plus, she could turn on her iPod while she worked, if she waited until she didn't have to hear anything. She finished up in dry storage, greeted her lunch cooks as they came in to set up the line and hustle the prep guys, then headed for her office.

Tuesdays were also schedule days. Next week was Valentine's Day. Every cook and dishwasher wanted it off, but she needed nearly every cook and at least two dishwashers. She decided to give her only married cook – Mikey -- the night off and to buy a bottle of something strong for the other guys. That'll buy them easily enough. Just as she put the finishing touches on the schedule, Monty popped his head in the office.

"Chef, I need . . . "

"No. I'll buy you some drinks, but you're here."

"Throw in a dime bag and it's a deal."

"I'm not buying you weed. Dinner for you and your girlfriend is on me Thursday. Ask for anything else and I will take it back."

"Deal."

He closed the door and Morrigan leaned back in her chair. These routines, this work, it was her home in the real world. It relaxed her. As she put her feet up on her desk, she could hear Monty flipping the light switch off outside of the office. She thought, "he needs a raise" and drifted off to sleep.

~~~~~~~~~~

"That is unpleasant." she thinks, as she looks out upon the macabre banquet table at which she sits with several others. The table is very long. In fact, she cannot see where it ends. She sits at the head of the table, which runs down what can only be described as a hallway. The walls of the hallway press against the sides of the table. The other occupants of the table are pinned, quite literally, between the walls and the table.

Large staples pierce the shoulders of the diners, blood pouring from the wounds they created as they went through the flesh and into the wood behind them. Barbed wire encircles their waists and stabs seamlessly into the floor. Their arms are free and they are using them to partake in the fare laid out before them.

Unlike the guests, the food is quite normal. It is laid out in pots and pans, not typical of a fancy feast, but it looks edible. Roasted meats and vegetables cover every spot on the table that isn't occupied by arms, hands, plates and flatware.

The tortured diners say nothing and reveal nothing of the pain they must be feeling as they delicately eat the food in front of them. Each of them uses their tools carefully in such a way that would leave an etiquette expert with nary a criticism. Morrigan is not phased by their injuries or their strange daintiness. She is used to such scenery in her nightmares. She would prefer it if they were free like her and finding some other way to be horrifying, but her dislike of their current situation is merely a passing unpleasantness.

Taking a cue from the wall ornaments, Morrigan begins to dine. Her nightmares are so vivid all the time that she is not surprised at all when she can taste the succulent chicken that she places in her mouth. She approves of the cuisine and sets about eating as much of it as she can.

When she has her fill, Morrigan turns to the closest diner on her right, a woman with brown curly hair plastered to her face by the sweat that is pouring from her skin. Morrigan asks her how her meal is.

"Uncomfortable, but quite delicious." The woman replies through her teeth. She almost spits the words at Morrigan, who doesn't so much as flinch.

"It liked it too, but I am finished. Do you know the way out of this place?"

"There is no way out of this place," a voice whispers. The sound comes from the darkness at the other end of the table. She thinks it must be one of the diners who is out of her field of vision.

"Well, I suppose we will have to make conversation until I wake," she replies.

Before the words can escape her mouth, there is the sound of rattling pans and pounding from whence the whispering voice had issued. A childlike figure with short, twisted arms materializes from the darkness, its small feet pounding on the table as it rushes toward Morrigan. It scoops up two pans as it comes, bashing the faces of the diners on either side of the table with them. None of them complains.

It's black eyes meet Morrigans and it screeched, "Scream." The word sounds like a plea. It is punctuated by the hitting of another diner. The things feet begin to move faster and its voice becomes louder. "Scream," thwap, "Scream," thunk "Screaaaaammmmmm." It reaches the end of the table and Morrigan sees that it is not a child, but a hairy dwarf of a man. He crouches, springs at Morrigan and presses his face against hers. His next words are delivered like a curse, spat directly into her face, "Do it! We are your horrors. Be horrified."

Morrigan can feel the oils of his face rubbing into her cheek. Her reply to his words ring as a command down the hall, "Remove your face!" His eyes spring open and he smiles slowly, as the walls shimmer and run like darkness from the light.

Disoriented, Morrigan awoke in her office.

Chapter 4

"Pay attention," he thinks.

Doctor Bateson had had a long day, but he listened to his favorite patient avidly, nonetheless. Morrigan had slept three nights since he last saw her. It made him feel bad about being groggy after only one bad night's sleep, but he couldn't help it. He was a hearty man, but he required eight solid hours of sleep per night or he was slightly disoriented. The fact that Morrigan had been in the very dream that made him sleep uneasily did not help his orientation, but he wasn't going to let his silly nightmare affect her session. She was paying a pretty penny to see him, after all.

"Do you recognize any of these characters you see in your dreams, Morrigan? I mean, apart from having seen some of them in previous dreams?"

"No. I have never seen any of them in movies, television or real life -- that I can recall."

"We've talked about this before, but I want to bring something else into the equation. We know that as far as modern dream investigation can tell us, we never see people in our dreams that we are not familiar with. We have always seen them before. Now, we also know that you do not remember a single person in any of your dreams. You have been keeping track of faces you notice in fleeting advertisements and such, correct?"

"Yes"

"And that has revealed nothing, thus far?"

"Again, not that I can recall."

"Have you ever pondered the possibility that you have repressed memories, Morrigan?"

"What?"

"Well, it's something that I usually do not delve into in my office because I don't like to encourage the forming of false memories through our discussions here. However, your insomnia, your anxiety and your nightmares filled with unfamiliar faces may point to a traumatic event that you have repressed. Perhaps those faces belong to people you forced yourself to forget. Your anxiety, night terrors and insomnia would fit right into past traumatic events."

The features of the Winged Man flashed in Morrigan's mind. No way. She would have remembered him. She never would have forgotten that face.

Morrigan knew the doc had an odd demeanor with his patients and that this candid discussion about potential sources for her maladies was a bit unusual, but that is why she stayed with him. She liked being privy to his thought process. It made her feel almost as if they were intimate friends instead of doctor and patient.

"I really don't think so, big guy. As you know, most of my life is recorded for all to see, apart from the first few years with my parents. After that, the home would have documented any traumatic event and I just really feel like nothing is missing after that. At least, nothing that could account for so many faces. Unless I was brutalized at a mass gathering and I sincerely doubt that."

"I did think about the sheer number of unfamiliar people in your dreams before mentioning it, Morrigan and I think I might have an idea. Perhaps these unfamiliar faces all represent one or a few people. It is possible that your dreaming mind applies different features to different characters that all stand for different aspects of one individual."

"I don't know, Doc. They all seem to be part of the same plot, as if put there by some storyteller, but they do not seem to be the same character. Take the difference between the dwarf man and the bound woman. One was aggressive and one was passive."

"Precisely. Besides, if the figures you dream up are really part of a single plot, then you are the storyteller as they all emit from your sleeping mind. I find it hard to believe that you are coming up with all of these characters on your own, with no outside stimuli and are the first to do so that we are aware of."

"Thanks, Doc."

"Don't be offended. You're a brilliant chef, but in an entire year, the only nickname you have come up with for me is Doc apart from the occasional big guy, which is not exactly at the top of the creativity ladder, considering it is a simple abbreviation for my title and a rather run of the mill comment on my size."

"Point taken, smart ass."

"Ah, there's a new one."

"Very professional."

"Back on track. You have said before that the nightmares seem to come from something other than yourself, like you are watching a movie and you know it is a movie, so it doesn't frighten you, but it doesn't feel like your movie. Does that still apply?"

The Winged Man entered her mind again. She hadn't seen him since his last, carnal appearance. Is he hers? "Yes," she thought, he is, "but not in the sense that I have created him."

"That seems to sum it up. If there is anything in there of my creation, it is too fleeting for me to feel it. I guess that is the gist of it. The nightmares must come from me, but so does this anxiety, so I guess I want to feel separated from them both."

"I wouldn't go so far. We can train ourselves to control certain aspects of dreams, but that is only because we already have control of them, we just don't know it when it is happening. What we do not do is control how we feel about our dreams. You should feel fear at nightmares, happiness at good dreams, befuddlement at strange dreams, etc. It's not as if we can all just change our natural reactions to things without ever even thinking about it or practicing it."

"What do you think, then?"

"I think we have wandered into the realm of analyzing your dreams and away from the realm of dealing with what it is that really ails you. Your night terrors are a symptom of something else and we have long felt that your anxiety and insomnia play a role in it, which is not uncommon for just plain anxiety disorders. There really is no need to analyze the dreams. What we need to analyze is you -- find a source and possibly deal with it enough to alleviate your stress and minimize your nightmares."

Stop the dreams? She had never thought of that as one of her goals. She was here to stop the anxiety attacks, the unreality, the discomfort upon waking and the insomnia. She liked to sleep. She didn't mind the nightmares. Of course, she had never told Doc that. She was afraid it was weird to feel unafraid by the things she saw.

Morrigan just always figured her calm in the face of nightmares was part and parcel of feeling like your dreams were a reality, but a fabricated one. Everything there, no matter how frightening an image, was benevolent. It couldn't hurt her. It was like a swearing and physically repulsive human being that is actually quite friendly, if you can look past the superficial shit. Even the violence in her dreams was carried out on those who didn't seem to mind. She wondered, though, what it would be like for her dreams to be here, in the real world.

"I don't know, Doc. I just want to find a connection between them and the anxiety."

"Stress."

"Baloney. We both know that as long as things go according to plan, I'm never stressed."

Tynan Bateson smiled crookedly.

"Morrigan, you may not think you are stressed because you are so given to the idiosyncrasies that dominate your personality, but you run at a constant high level. You only notice it when you have anxiety because it is the only way stress can register with someone like you."

"So, what do you think? I need a vacation?"

"That would be good. We could at least try something of the sort and see what kind of effect it has on you."

Morrigan sighed heavily. "We'll talk about it next time. Looks like it is time for me to go to work and for you to go wherever you troll yourself away at night."

"We'll talk more about this vacation next week."

She was already up and walking out the door, prepared to ignore his demand.

"Yep, have a good week."

Tynan walked over to his bookshelf when he heard the door click shut. From the shelf, he plucked a thick, brown leather volume marked only by gold Roman numerals. He plopped it open on his desk and thumbed through the pages. He did not find what he was looking for, so he put the book back, grabbed his coat and walked out of his office, completely unaware that Morrigan would have recognized one of the illustrations he came across in the book, though he likely would have thought she had seen it before, was lying or was crazy -- her Winged Man.

~~~~~~~~~

"Order up!" Monty spun the plate into the window with a finesse that showed his years of playing with plates in kitchens. "Dinner was great, Chef. The latest Monty sperm bank dug your fancy schmancy dining room."

"Sperm bank?' Morrigan replied. "You mean she actually let you dip that pathetic thing in her?" She glanced down to the crotch area of his checkered chef pants.

"Right after dinner." Monty emphasized this by thrusting his pelvis against the stainless steel work station.

"I'm not paying for it when she sues you for violating whatever law I'm sure you violated."

"The only thing she'll sue me for is more."

Morrigan laughed and looked up at the clock. Her staff was already eying her impatiently, knowing that saying something would only get them stuck here. Morrigan wasn't in the mood to fuck with them tonight. "86 the kitchen please!" she shouted out the window. A glance through the porthole showed that Christine was getting ready to put in a food order. Without even looking at the kitchen she turned back to the man from whom she was taking an order, leaned over until her cleavage was at eye level and offered him a dessert instead. "Thatta girl," Morrigan thought and began breaking down the kitchen.

Morrigan walked home from the restaurant, despite the time, as she did every Friday night. The streets were dotted with the more sinister denizens of the city, but she had never feared being accosted on her walk home. Perhaps it was her height and confident stature, but she had never been bothered by anyone, save Doomsey. She was nearing his corner when she began to feel the dreaded panic wash over her. She walked faster, as if she could outrun it. Just as she approached the intersection where the crazy homeless man sat and where she hooked a left to her apartment, he came into view. She stopped short.

This was different! The panic now came in waves, numbing her limbs and making her teeth chatter. "Fuck, fuck, fuck," she thought. Standing next to a sitting Doomsey was a small, dwarfish man with an oily face. He banged two pots together, saying, "You will all scream, scream, scream when the end comes." He looked at Morrigan and laughed. "You won't scream, will you?" He began to shuffle toward her. It was then that she found her momentum and ran. "You won't. You won't. You won't," he shouted after her between giggles.

Morrigan heard Doomsey say as she ran away, "Maybe she will bring you coffee tomorrow too." This only man the dwarf man laugh harder.

When Morrigan reached her apartment, she ran to the bathroom where she lay, sure she would vomit, for 20 minutes. When the vomit never came, she decided to curl up on the couch with a heating blanket to make the shaking subside. She considered calling Dr. Bateson, but knew there was nothing he could do for her. She lay there shaking and not sleeping for six hours.

Later, she slipped into a dreamless sleep that ended with her deciding that a vacation was exactly the right thing for her. Monty could handle it. The anxiety exhausted her. There was nothing else to be done.

Chapter 5

The following Saturday, Morrigan was in her old GMC pickup truck headed for Logan Airport. Monty was in full control of the restaurant and, oddly, Morrigan was not in the least bit worried about it. She was a little apprehensive about her trip, but had every detail planned down to the time of her meals, though most of the trip was free time to roam around in the snow. She chuckled as she recalled Doc's reaction to her travel plans the day before.

"Let me get this straight. I tell you to go on vacation and you decide to go to the Arctic Circle in February? You do realize I meant for you to have stress relief to get these night terrors to slow down, right?"

Morrigan had outright laughed at him. She was in unnaturally high spirits. She was getting excited about her trip, yes, but she was also excited to leave the dwarf man behind. He had been with Doomsey every day since that first night. Morrigan hated to give in to her uneasiness, but she had not bothered to buy Doomsey coffee at all. He was certainly affected, as he had begun mixing colorful obscenities in with his usual curses. Christine was making up for it by bringing both the dwarf man and Doomsey coffee on Morrigan's dime, but that didn't change a thing. He looked at her with contempt and she couldn't help but feel like she deserved it. Whatever the reason for this bizarre change of character, she was excited that she wouldn't have to think about it for two weeks.

"Doc, I have not been on vacation in, let's see, my whole life. If I'm doing it, I'm going to do something I have always wanted to do."

". . . and that is view the Aurora Borealis from an ice igloo in Finland?"

"Yes, in a roundabout way. It's mostly about the novelty of it and the lights."

Morrigan had always imagined the Aurora Borealis at night to be something like her painting of the darkness. She had the feeling it would suit her quite well.

"As long as you relax, I am on board, Morrigan." He said the words, but he still shook his head. Morrigan got the sense that he didn't like the distance, the layovers and the cold. To him, it didn't sound like a de-stressor for a beautiful, slender woman in her mid-twenties, but he would take a grueling vacation over no vacation at all. He really did care about her and wanted her to feel better.

By the time Morrigan got on the first plane on her three plane journey to the hotel in Finland, she felt the eerie dissimilitude between herself and her daily environment melting away. She knew she would feel some unease at the hotel, but she felt like the whitewashed landscape and the black night sky above her igloo would help with some of that. The cluttered and commercial beaches of just about any tropical vacation were part of the reason she was going to Finland. She had thought about Iceland, but figured she would save it until some summer so she could go by boat.

The flight and subsequent hours long trip to the hotel, which was in the northernmost part of Finland, took Morrigan more than a day. She did not sleep. She did crossword puzzles and listened to her iPod, but most of all, she drew. She drew the banquet table she saw in her dream the week before. She drew the dwarf man with his pots and stomping feet. She drew a black river surrounded by iridescent red grass that she saw in her nightmares a few nights before. She drew the Winged Man, who still eluded her. She drew him as she had always known him -- beautiful, malevolent-looking, but safe to her. She did not draw him as he was on the night he had managed to make her feel uncomfortable. The last thing she needed was a self-induced anxiety attack nearly 10,000 miles from home.

She put her suitcases on the floor, next to the bed in her glass igloo. She put her carry on on the bed, removing the important items such as toothbrush, hairbrush and iPod. She removed her jacket, hat, gloves, sweater and two scarves from her suitcases before plugging the ear buds for her iPod into her ears. She then carried her toothbrush and toothpaste into the bathroom beside the door where she had entered the igloo. Brushing her teeth felt excellent, as did removing her pants and shirt when she finished. It was odd for her stripping down in a glass hotel room that is completely exposed to the outside in every direction, but she was assured that it wasn't as revealing as she thought, not that peeping toms particularly freaked her out. She was used to feeling watched.

Morrigan had a few hours before nightfall, so she decided to take a hot shower, get dressed and see what there was to do around the resort. The shower warmed her up enough to allow her to venture back out into the cold. After checking the information packet on the table near the door for a restaurant, she made sure her hair was completely dry before braiding it and tucking it into her hat. She wore a cozy brown sweater and leggings beneath a pair of jeans. She also wore wool socks beneath a pair of sturdy snow boots. She hoped that bundling up was the way to go and that she wouldn't stick out among the rugged Finlanders. As it turned out, she didn't.

She chose to dine at the most interesting of the restaurants available at the resort -- The Snow Restaurant. She had read about before coming to Finland

and knew that it was the largest such restaurant in the world and really a rare treat. Upon walking in, she could see why they called it The Snow Restaurant. The bar was made of ice and the entire restaurant was made of snow. She was seated in a small table against the back wall by an polite hostess who asked for her drink order. Morrigan ordered a whiskey and a coke, separate.

While she sat there, so far from home, Morrigan began to feel lonely. It wasn't a common feeling for her, given that she had been without family most of her life and living alone for her entire adult life. She ate her food, having only cursory interactions with her server. The food was excellent; not what she expected. After dinner, she checked out the ice gallery at the resort and wandered back to her igloo. In the mood to really relax, she ordered a bottle of Jack Daniels from room service, plugged her iPod into her ears and lay back on the bed. It wasn't quite dark yet, but it was nearing time for Morrigan to enjoy what she had come here for.

As she lay there, she drifted off into a brief, dreamless sleep. About ten minutes had passed when a light tap on the door woke Morrigan from her rest. The sun was setting, but color still painted the sky. She opened the door to a kind hotel employee who gave her the bottle, as well as glasses and ice. He politely asked if she needed anything else and reminded her of perks, such as a hot sauna, that she could take advantage of. She thanked him, tipped him, closed the door and poured a hefty glass of the charcoal tinted liquor.

Her loneliness had subsided, for the most part, and excitement for the night's entertainment had settled in. It was time to strip off the jeans, for it was cozy in the igloo. She curled up with a pillow, plugged the iPod back into her ears and waited patiently for one of the few things she had always wanted to see. Trees marred her vision from the sides, but the roof gave an excellent view of the sky, marred only by the black bars that held the glass panes in place.

It was not long until darkness settled. Every light in the glass igloo was extinguished. Even the iPod light was obscured by the blanket Morrigan tucked it under. Here was the comfort she had come here to find. The darkness, the isolation. Even the sparse furnishings of her igloo and the very shape of it made the real world less unreal. She never thought about the fact that igloos are shaped like nightmares and dreams. Even if she would have thought of it, she didn't have time.

"Holy shit."

The light show began. Morrigan watched as the colors played in the sky. Predominantly green wisps of color with some red lit up the night. Beyond and between the wisps of color, the stars were clearer than she had ever seen them. She reminded herself to photograph the event tomorrow, so she could hang the photographs in the restaurant and maybe share some. She marveled at how the tops of the trees were black against the sky, but that she could see the details of their branches and needles. She felt like she was in one of her nightmares, but all alone, which almost never happened. It was like being alone in your favorite place, no background noise, no one to steal your attention. Just you and an environment that feels like home. There was no denying it. She loved it here and, for the next 12 days, she was sure she wouldn't feel lonely again.

After two hefty drinks, a drunken stumble to sauna land and another half hour of staring up at the sky, Morrigan drifted to sleep.

Chapter 6

Morrigan had once read somewhere about the Sarah Winchester house. People claimed that it was ever changing and growing stranger due to a crew of ghostly workers who could be heard continuing construction on the house long past the time that they and the owner of the house were dead. Stairways that led to nowhere, hidden rooms, etc. Morrigan had found the house interesting, as she always did the things that seemed to have slipped from someone's nightmare into the real world.

The house in which she walked now was much more strange, constantly changing and nightmarish than the Sarah Winchester house because it wasn't presented in the real world. It is part of her nightmare and therefore exponentially more nightmarish. The walls are red and peeling. They all tilt in toward the top, as if they are about to fall in on her. There are doors everywhere. She keeps opening them and walking through without paying attention to where she is going. It would not have mattered anyway, if she had, nothing ever looks the same if she concentrates on it. She has to go with the flow or lose the scenery.

A series of doorways gets larger and larger as she passes through them, leading her to a circular ballroom. In the center of the ballroom sits a gilded salt throne, adorned with lapis lazuli. She is drawn to it, she wants to sit there, but she remembers a similar salt throne from her childhood that people said was haunted. They heard horrible screams and felt invisible entities touching them around the salt throne of her childhood. It is their distaste of the haunted chair that keeps Morrigan from this one, despite her lack of fear.

The room grows marginally brighter than it had been when she walked in. She looks around and notices suits of armor lining the walls.

"What an odd choice for ballroom decor," she says aloud.

"Would you prefer the decor of the dining room?" The familiar voice comes from behind her. Weary of their last encounter, she turns to face the Winged Man. He is clothed and smiling at her, his green eyes dancing over her face and body. She wonders what he is looking at. As soon as the thought enters her mind, he is standing behind her, his arms around her waist, turning her to face a mirror that pokes through between two very grotesque and decidedly oriental suits of armor.

On her skin is the turquoise gown that the tree woman had worn when last Morrigan had dreamed of the Winged Man. Like the woman, it is easy to see

Morrigan's entire body through the gown. It flows like Spartan robes underwater, as if some current moves the material against her skin. She can feel the movement and finds it stimulating in ways unfamiliar to her. A blue aurora against her skin. How fitting.

"It doesn't mean you have to stare." She says petulantly, taking his meaning, though he had not spoken.

"That's exactly what it means, but let's not linger on trivialities, Morrigan. It seems you will be asleep for some time, thanks to your friend Jack." He smiles his disarming smile, lined with perfect white teeth. "What would you like to do?"

"How do you know that?"

"Didn't your doctor tell you? All of this comes from your mind, including me. I know because you know."

"I don't believe that."

"Ah, trivialities again. You're going to bore me."

"Then go away. I'll manage to amuse myself without you." She says this last scathingly. It is unlike them to have such conversations. When they talk, which they had often in the past, they speak of the landscape, nightmarish props, etc. They never speak of each other. It is as if each pretends the other is a nonentity.

"Morrigan, I will leave you to wander these pits of morbidity by yourself, if you wish." He sounds angry and the buzzing of bees begin to emit from the suits of armor, though no insects are present. It is an enraged and all-encompassing sound.

"I wish to sit there." She points to the salt throne and the Winged Man shrugs, the black feathers of his wings rustling as he does so.

"So sit, Queen Morrigan."

She scoffs. "Queen. Aren't we acting strange today?"

"Every day is strange, Morrigan. Sit on the throne." He removes his arms from her waist and takes two steps back.

Morrigan walks weightlessly to the throne, her aurora dress caressing her as she walks. She opens the compartment where she knew salt would have been placed long ago and is surprised to see salt in it. The bees buzz even louder. She turns to the Winged Man and he glares at her impatiently. In a moment of inspiration, Morrigan grabs a handful of salt from the compartment and tosses it toward the Winged Man.

Screams erupt everywhere. "Hmm," she thinks, "they were right." The screams are the screams of the tortured. Truly horrible sounds. The salt moves through the air slowly. She can see each granule individually as it moves, glinting off the light. In the sparks of light, she sees people, tortured souls of every description -- a mother holding her dead infant, a soldier alone amidst the mangled bodies of his fallen comrades, a jealous husband crying over his murdered wife's body. Thousands of them, screaming and telling Morrigan their stories. They are saying, "Welcome to our nightmare, Morrigan. Go ahead and make them worse."

As she watches, fascinated by the stories being told, the Winged Man gestures in the air, moving the grains of salt back into the salt compartment. Morrigan watches him complete the task and then shuts the lid.

"They do not need you to remind them, Morrigan. Just sit." She does. The buzzing stops. The walls begin to right themselves, the peeling on the walls begins healing like wounds. The decay of the house is vanishing, but as it does, the house becomes even more sinister and nightmarish. The shapes of faces press against the red walls as if it were some macabre womb. Spiders scuttle into the corners, as if even they are intimidated by the dwelling in which they reside. The house itself lets forth a howling yawn. Cracking is heard throughout before it settles into a more regal position. The armor is again shiny. In some places, blood drips through the cracks in the glistening metal. The hands of the suits remove weapons long since lodged in the metal and whatever monstrosities lay within.

"Interesting, isn't it?" He stretches his wings and then tucks them back behind himself.

"What just happened?"

"I suppose you can call it something like a homecoming. It doesn't matter right now. It just is. Come with me."

She looks at him and decides at once that he is the draw for her. Not these strange occurrences. When she sleeps, she wants to spend time with him, so she goes with him. He locks his legs and arms around her body and flies them out of the house through a maze of hallways. Morrigan has just enough time to notice the bloody arms reaching for her through some of the floors, the groups of macabre characters that huddled in various areas of the house, committing random acts of violence on each other and the house itself making greedy noises like it has begun to dine.

They fly through absolutely black nothingness until they reach a body of star lit water over which the Winged Man flies them. Upon looking closer above and below, Morrigan sees that it is not stars reflecting off the water, there is something happening beneath the water. Figures move about below the pristine surface; the lights are coming from them. Then, the water is gone. They are in a stone castle carved from a cliff on the water's edge. The Winged Man places her on the floor in what can only be described as a massive foyer. He holds her hand and walks her up a white marble staircase in the center of the room.

As he walks, he talks to Morrigan, "It's time to start something more than this cycle you have going in your life, Morrigan. You have to start adjusting to who you really are and stop with this fear garbage."

She tries to remove her hand from his, "I'm not afraid. I believe I just showed you that."

He laughs loudly and ruthlessly. "Please, Morrigan. I know you are not afraid here, though you could make things quite a bit more frightening. You're afraid when you are awake. You tiptoe through everything but your business with the air of some obsessive compulsive coward. You don't understand, so you conform to societal norms." His hand releases hers and he walks on ahead of her. "This doesn't make sense to me, so I'll seek therapy. I see things other people do not see in the same way, so I resort to panicking. Really, Morrigan. It's getting pathetic."

She feels a wrath that she has never felt before well up inside of her. When her voice issues forth from her body, she can hardly recognize it. It has the commanding tone she heard in the dining room when speaking to the dwarf man, but there is something more, something guttural. "Fuck you. I made you. You are a part of my mind, so behave in a manner that pleases me or disappear. I don't care to be made fun of by my own imagination."

If she thought the laughter was bad before, it was ten times worse now. "Oh, Morrigan. That was adorable. Quite impressive, really, but still adorable. I am not a part of your mind. Where we stand is not a part of your mind either. Sure, you push what you see in your nightmares, making it nearly impossible for you to even have a dream, but really, imagine the hubris of thinking I am your creation. You're not that creative, darling." The last was said with a rough edge to his voice, as if he was determined to prove to her that her anger was powerless against him, that the control she always craved was not hers to have with him. He would make her very uncomfortable and she would learn to cope with it. She had to.

He grabs her around the upper legs with one arm and flings her over his back. His other hand finds its way beneath her gown in ten ways before she even has a moment to think. He is carrying her up the stairs, touching her as if she belongs to him in some way and she can't shake the feeling that he is teaching her a lesson, helping her learn her place, though she also has the faint notion that he and she are on equal footing in many ways.

A hallway, a door, they were through both and into an expansive, gilded and white bedroom for only a second before his free hand finds a way to violate her. One long finger is inside her for a split second before he throws her on the bed. She tries to move away, but he spreads his wings and makes a cocoon around their upper torsos with them. His finger does not leave her as he curls and releases it in a come hither motion that teases her into arousal.

"Fuck, stop it."

"No. This is a dream. Enjoy it and wake up happy later."

"It doesn't feel like a dream."

"Even better."

The wings are gone and his face is moving toward his finger. She stops struggling, though she wonders why he hast kissed her yet. Just as the thought crosses her mind, he kisses her with his warm lips and tongue, but not where she expects. He continues the come hither motion with his finger until she lets go, violently shaking. He lifts his face to hers, but still does not kiss her.

"See? We'll do that in one of your nightmares next time."

She can feel his hardness against the inside of her thigh and wonders if he will have sex with her here on this bed. Instead, he rubs it against her, clearly becoming more excited with every moment.

"Why aren't you . . .?"

He shakes his head against her neck. "Not now, Morrigan."
"At least let me help you."

His head snaps up, his eyes wide and excited. She can tell had not expected this. Ah, so they are on equal footing in some ways.

Before he can say anything, she reaches her hand down between him and wraps it around his impressive penis. She rubs slowly at first, using the moisture dripping out of both of them to slicken his skin. She rolls him beneath her, his breathing now heavy and uneven. She moves to return the favor with her mouth, but realizes there is no way he will fit. Instead, she laps at him, still moving her hand. His hips begin to thrust with her motion until he finally grips her shoulders, stopping her.

Morrigan wakes up.

Chapter 7

Morrigan woke to the sun streaming into the igloo. It was the brightest morning she had seen in a long time. There was no escaping the light. She sighed and thought, "I'll have to make do with this." Sitting up, she realized that the clothing she fell asleep in was no longer on her body. She looked around and noticed the bottle of whiskey she started last night was half-empty and open on the shelf that ran along the edge of the wall, in lieu of furniture. Pondering her inexplicable lack of clothing, Morrigan wrapped the sheet around her body and made her way to the bathroom.

As she walked, she could feel a warm wetness between her legs. Now red and flustered, Morrigan tried to ignore the fact that her dream had so affected her. She wandered back into the bedroom area, discarded the sheet, grabbed her bathrobe and went into the bathroom. Steam from the shower moistened her skin as stood in front of the mirror, taking note of the night's damage. The mirror reflected back a red face, slightly puffy from sleep. She ran a brush through her hair, fighting with tangles as the steam from the shower obscured her reflection. The bathrobe fell to the floor as she stepped into the shower.

~~~~~~~~~~

"Hold on back there," the guide said in what Morrigan thought of as garbled, happy English. The apparatus bumped over the packed in snow as the reindeer pulled Morrigan and an American family of four through the forest. She had felt a little out of place, at first, but once the mom got to chatting, Morrigan mostly started feeling sorry for herself. She tucked her hands away under her legs and periodically pinched herself as a reminder to pay attention to what the woman was saying and nod at the appropriate moments.

"Our oldest didn't come with us because he didn't want to take the time off college. I just cooked up a storm in anticipation so the darling wouldn't starve to death." The woman's red curls bobbed against her cheeks and fought with her hat as she spoke. "He told me he has a lot of studying to do and to stop worrying about him, but I just can't help it. He's such a good kid at college with some other good kids, but I have spotted some evildoers among them. Mark my words, some of those boys are going to get some good boys in trouble this year. Darn shame, if you ask me." As the chubby, excitable woman talked about her saintly son, Morrigan pictured a younger, male version of her taking bong hits and listening to heavy metal in some dorm room in Jesus country. At least he wouldn't have to worry about spraying his clothes before going to church with his mom today.

"Do you have any kids?' The woman's voice broke into Morrigan's amused imaginings.

"What? Oh, kids. No, I don't have any kids."

The woman eyes became slits of suspicion. Morrigan shifted in her seat and wondered what she did to upset the woman. Despite herself, Morrigan made excuses for her childless state. "You see, I run my own business and don't want to settle down until the place has learned to take care of itself."

Another suspicious look. "Ohhh, what kind of business?'

"Not a fishing one, you nosy bitch." Morrigan thought. "Ohhh" she said, in a pretty good mockery of the woman's voice that went undetected. "I run a Greek restaurant in the city."

"That sounds like fun."

A thin, wet smile spread across the woman's face. She kept her eyes on Morrigan for what seemed like too long. In the meantime, her family looked down, apparently happy that they were not the recipients of her false niceties. It sounded like her idea of fun was hosting a dinner party with her morose-looking husband and long suffering children as the main decor for the event. Morrigan was not far off. The woman had spent the morning in their igloo reminding her children of their inadequacies before embarking on their adventure.

"It is fun." Morrigan said, deciding to just pretend this was like any other conversation. "The restaurant is nominally successful. I have a decent reputation and a heap of regulars. It really couldn't be better."

She was being completely honest. The restaurant was in tip top shape. Her staff was great, her clientele was great, her reviews were great. It was the rest of her life that was in the pits. Even her nightmares were becoming an oddity, something she wasn't used to, though the moment she thought of it, a jolt of pleasure shot through her. "Ugh, that's awkward." she thought.

"You still have time for a family. You're not that old."

Morrigan's posture straightened. What was she supposed to say to this daft woman? "Oh, I have never been in a relationship because change in my life makes me crazy. The idea of having to compromise with another human being makes my palms sweat and I would rather hang myself than wind up like you."

She couldn't say that.

Morrigan huffed, "Hmm. Maybe." With this, she looked away from the woman and her family, effectively ending the conversation.

Morrigan looked out at the landscape. There was snow in every direction, but it was the subtle way it seemed to run up the trunks of trees in places and kiss the edges of streams that enchanted Morrigan. It really was beautiful, something it would be hard for even the weird lady to ruin. She wondered what the lady would think if she knew about the way Morrigan's mind functioned. What would she say if they took a lovely day trip into the recesses of one of Morrigan's nightmares? She was willing to bet that the woman had never had a nightmare about anything more grotesque than a fallen cake in the oven. Her mind conjured intrusive images of the women thrashing about in the black river, dining with barbed wire around her body, screaming in a grain of salt. Somewhere the Winged Man laughed.

~~~~~~~~~~

For two days, it was much like that second day. Morrigan went on day trips with other tourists, ice sculpting, eating, checking out Santa's village and kicking back in the sauna. She didn't fall asleep the second night, but the third night found her sleeping for roughly four hours. She was back where you could see through the grass and it glowed red. She just sat there, alone, on the edge of the black river, watching indescribable shapes burst up in the blackness from time to time, always unable to break the surface, but able to disturb it.

The Winged Man sits on the other side of the river, up a hill. He says nothing and he does not move, save to ruffle his wings from time to time. Morrigan makes no attempt to approach him. She is alone in her world. If he wants to watch, that is fine, but she doesn't want to spend her entire vacation processing her dreams and she was starting to think that her mind would not let things go back to normal with her and the Winged Man, given that she had already taken it to the next level -- or had she? He had explicitly said that he was not her creation. Who was he then? She shook her head to chase away the thoughts and relaxed for the rest of her brief dream.

~~~~~~~~~~

After two days of nothing special, Morrigan rode a van filled with non-English speaking tourists into town. She dressed as well as she could in a maroon cowl necked sweater, tight gray pants and black boots to her knees. She wore her black hair straight down, but had to top it with a red and black knit hat.

For three hours, she roamed the small shops in town, thumbing through crisp new books and perusing shelves of shiny knick-knacks that would one day adorn shelves in countries around the world. She purchased a few books about the aurora borealis in one of the few bookstores that did not also contain sweatshirts, t-shirts, baseball caps and bumper stickers. She was also able to find presents for her cooks, Christine and Doc, who she was starting to regret being away from for more than a week. The shutter on her camera worked overtime as she walked from store to store and wondered what it would be like to live in such a place. Finally, her stomach growled loud enough for her to imagine that passersby were hearing it and she went in search of a restaurant.

She had been walking down a shop-lined street and decided to take a left at the intersection up ahead to see what that street had to offer in the way of food. Her toe caught the edge some packed snow as she turned the corner. The resulting stumble threw her into what felt like a brick wall.

Morrigan looked up and saw that the wall was a person, a gigantic person with green eyes, black hair and an indistinguishable accent.

"Excuse me. Did I hurt you?'

"No, no. I'm so sorry. I tripped and . . . "

"Yes, I saw." He laughed.

As he laughed, the lines of the man's face revealed a rugged handsomeness. The corners of his full mouth pulled up to reveal deep dimples in his chiseled cheeks. The thick flannel and stiff-looking jeans he wore did nothing to detract from his overall appealing appearance.

Morrigan couldn't help but notice how handsome he was. His features were similar to those of the Winged Man, but it was no competition. This man was real, human, he couldn't live up to a man with wings who only existed in nightmares. Nonetheless, Morrigan felt a tickle of desire as she looked up into his friendly face.

Morrigan Fuseli had lived most of her life without feeling anything more than friendly attraction to real people. She never told anyone, but she had absolutely no romantic experience, despite numerous offers both in college and at her restaurant. Her inexperience flashed through her mind and she shook it off, thinking, "For fuck's sake, Morrigan. As if that matters. You bumped into each other. You didn't make arrangements to have sex on the ground in the street." That thought didn't help. "All right, idiot, say something," she thought.

"I was just looking for a restaurant. I'm sorry again. I won't keep you." Her boots splashed in the slush that covered the edges of the sidewalk as she began walking away.

He called after her, "Unless you plan on eating at someone's house, you are going in the wrong direction."

The splashing stopped and she turned to look back at him.

"You'll want to go this way." He pointed down the street toward where she would have been, had she taken a right at the intersection.

"Oh, thank you." She began splashing in the other direction, avoiding the dry center of the sidewalk so she would not have to get too close to him.

"You should really get a map."

"I planned on winging it. I hear I do not do that often enough." she gave a tentative laugh at her own expense. To her surprise, he smiled.

"I hear the opposite. Come here. I will walk you to the best place in town." He gestured for her to walk beside him.

"Oh, no. That's okay. I'm sure I can find it."

"I'm going there anyway. It is dinner time, after all. Besides, now, if we don't walk together, we will just walk awkwardly in the same direction until we both reach our destination and awkwardly enter at the same time, but not together."

She saw his point. It was a good one.

"All right."

As they walked, she asked what kind of restaurant they were going to and happily learned that it was authentic local cuisine. She wondered aloud if they had the salmon soup she kept hearing about it and learned that they did.

"You'll want to try the reindeer, though." he looked at her as if hoping impishly if that would garner a typical American reaction like, "Oh, no. You can't eat Santa's helpers." Instead, she said, "I plan on it."

By the time they reached the door of the restaurant with a name that seemed rife with misplaced vowels and consonants, the two had built up a repertoire that worked for both of them.

"I'm Eric, by the way," he said as they walked in.

"Morrigan" she reached out her hand to shake his.

"Morrigan, that is a very interesting name. Have dinner with me," he replied without skipping a beat.

Before she could change her mind, she gave a rushed, "Sure."

When they had finished their twin salmon soups and were awaiting their reindeer, the conversation went from stories about their trips (he was also traveling) and wandered into a more personal zone.

"So what do you do for a living, Eric?"

"You're looking at."

One of Morrigan's eyebrows lifted.

"That's right. I pick up beautiful American women on the streets of freezing foreign countries and ask them out to dinner. That was a carefully placed chunk of ice you tripped on, by the way." he winked at her.

Baffled at the flirty talk that didn't involve swearing and humping kitchen appliances, Morrigan did her best to keep up.

"You're lucky it wasn't a man who tripped over your trap then."

"That would have landed me a fishing buddy at least, but I do admit to preferring this." His relaxed postured showed that he was quite at ease as he said this and Morrigan was afraid her inexperience was showing like the eponymous nose of the most famous of the soon-to-be dined upon ruminants. She took a deep breath and told herself that she just had to get through this, which was pleasant enough, and then she could go lie in bed and enjoy the aurora.

"Okay, seriously. I write travel guides, so I travel a lot. I just finished a guide in Rio de Janeiro. This is a shock to the system." That explained his tan.

"That sounds, well, I'll be honest, that sounds awful." She laughed. "I probably would not enjoy the chaos of constant travel."

"Well, I do meticulously plan. It is my job to get this stuff right. What do you do for a living?"

"I'm a chef and restaurant owner." His laughter rang through the small restaurant. "What's so funny?"

"I was a line cook in France for two years."

"You're hired. I still don't see what is funny," she stuck her tongue out at him. Very uncharacteristic.

He mimicked her voice, "'I probably would not enjoy the chaos . . .' and you're a chef. Do you run the slowest restaurant in the United States?"

"No. I'm just the best chef in the United States."

"And humble too."

The conversation went on like this through dessert and a round of digestifs. They discussed family. His was large, hers nonexistent. They discussed home life, hers was scarce and his was nonexistent. He didn't even have an apartment, to her surprise.

"No sense in renting while I'm writing on location." he had said in response to her shock.

Surprising herself, Morrigan told him about her anxiety and how this vacation was supposed to help and said that it seemed like, so far, it had. He seemed sympathetic. He said that he dealt with his stress after college by traveling, which had later transferred to this job. He said he had gone to school to be a doctor, got half way through and realized that regardless of the reward, he hated seeing people in pain, so he had dropped out. Had Morrigan had more experience with intimate interactions, she would have realized he was lying, especially about his sentiments.

After a fight over the check that Eric won, they opened the door to a rush of cold wind and were greeted by the night sky.

"It looks so much better over my room." Morrigan said. "It's beautiful here, but there is something about the lack of artificial light that makes it special."

"You should show me." he said, putting his hand on the small of her back.

Morrigan had no wish to really get to know this man. She had no wish to be intimate with him, but wishes are funny in that even when we wish something won't happen, whether the wish is right or wrong, it can happen anyway. Instead of being herself and declining this man's suggestion, she tried to sound casual as she said, "sure," and allowed him to lead her to his rental truck. On the ride to the hotel, his hand rested hotly on her leg as he talked with her.

He looked over at her, almost leering at her in the dimly lit truck cab. "I'm surprised to have met someone like you here -- so smart and absolutely gorgeous. You would be surprised at how few interesting people there are in this world."

Morrigan took the compliment with a grain of salt. She was not one to soak in flattery. She had decided to spend some time with the man, let him in her room, see where things went, as if she knew anything about that other than from dreams. However, she wasn't going to let this get all heady. She had roughly a week left in Finland and she wasn't going to spend it all with this writer, no matter how sexy he was.

She smiled and he looked away, giving her a chance to look at him in profile. He really was quite handsome, still not the man of her nightmares, but very easy on the eyes. She looked down his long, muscular body and noticed the bulge of his pants was decidedly sticking out. Her face turned red and she tried to look away. He made no effort to conceal it and showed no embarrassment. Instead, he moved his hand up her leg. Her first instinct was to stop this whole thing from happening. She had not been expecting this. However, she made a mental pact with herself. If she was going to try to be normal and make her life normal, she had to do what Doc said, be spontaneous, in so many words. This is what single woman her age do.

She slid down a little in the seat so his hand moved even farther up enough for him to feel the warmth between her legs. He let out a small chuckle that sounded suspiciously like a groan. "Morrigan, you are amazing." His hips moved like he couldn't help it, but he took his hand off her and asked her to direct him to where they needed to go. "I have to get us there in one piece." he laughed

They managed to get to Morrigan's room and pour a couple of drinks from the bottle Morrigan had abandoned on the first night before they resumed their previous touching. Eric sat on the bed and pulled her toward him. She straddled his hips as he lifted up her shirt and began kissing her stomach. This was more than anything Morrigan had ever experienced. She leaned across him and took a long pull from her drink. It was definitely starting to get a little overwhelming. She could feel his hardness through her pants and wondered if she was making a bad choice.

In a single motion, he stood up with one arm holding her in position and his other arm pulling her shirt over her head. She wore no bra, as she had small enough breasts to get away with it. His hot mouth covered a nipple as his now free hand found its way down the back of her pants, delving past her buttocks, his fingers found the warm moisture in her panties. He softly laughed his groaning laugh again. While he fondled her skillfully, they kissed. Their mouths found each other's mouths, necks, ears and shoulders, until they separated long enough for Eric to lay Morrigan on the bed on her stomach, lift her against his crotch and pull her pants off. With her face down and her behind in the air, she had never felt so vulnerable and somehow rebellious, despite that she had no one to rebel against.

Morrigan started to roll over on her back, but Eric pushed her down with his torso as he removed his pants and boxers. She could feel him against her backside the moment he freed his penis. She lay there and let him rub it on the outside of her panties. This was less work than she thought it would be and she thought she might be enjoying it, despite a nagging sense of having made a mistake. She could feel warm moisture soaking her panties. He groaned as he felt it too.

"I can feel your hot pussy juice through your panties. Uhh,"

Morrigan's stomach started to roll in revulsion. The familiar numbness of panic began to creep over her.

He rubbed his cock on the outside of her, every now and then giving a tentative poke, letting her feel the tip of his dick getting a little purchase through the thin material.

"I could cum doing this, but I really want to fuck you."

She heard a package tear as he opened a condom. In the back of her mind, she was hoping he wasn't planning on pushing on her underwear much longer, so she pulled her panties down herself. She was in full panic mode now and just wanted this over so he would leave. This was all the invitation he needed. He grabbed her hips and thrust himself into her.

A few minutes of writhing on top of her later, Eric noticed a little bit of bleeding.

"Morrigan, I think you have your period."

She knew it was coming. "No I do not."

He stopped dead. "You're a virgin?'

"I was."

"That's awesome," and he continued what he was doing for a few minutes before stopping again. "I want your ass too."

"What?'

"I want your ass too." then it dawned on her and she knew she didn't want to go any further. She had already had her fill of the unknown and didn't feel any intimacy with Eric anymore after listening to him grunt over her.

"No, Eric." she felt him slip out of her.

"Too late." and then the pain. It ripped through her. She had no preparation, no time to breathe. His hand clamped down over her mouth in anticipation of her scream. Morrigan was unsurprised to find that she felt no anger, no disgust, no emotions. She was empty except for the pain. She had never expected anything more from this reality, where her "self" was so fragile, where nothing seemed real.

The unreality swooped down to save her from this horrid violation. She felt gone, though she could hear him sweating and feel him pumping into her until he reached climax. Sure she wasn't struggling, he released her mouth and pulled out of her.

"Thank you," he said. She said nothing. "Mind if I use your shower?" She said nothing. "Fine, be like that."

He dressed himself while Morrigan lay there staring at the glass walls. She heard him leave without a word and let out a sigh of relief before rolling onto her back and letting pain course through her. Naked and oblivious, she walked to the door and locked it. Then, she cleaned off her glass of Jack and his, grabbed the bottle and went into the bathroom.

Chapter 8

"Morrigan."

The voice of the Winged Man carries across a field of the blood grass. She lies there in the field, staring at the veins in the grass, marveling at the drops of her own blood that appear on her hands as she sweeps her fingers across the blades. The droplets fall and are absorbed by the greedy vegetation. She is holding her arm up and watching the blood from the wounds in her hand pour down when the Winged Man sweeps her off the ground, sits down and holds her in his lap like a sleeping baby.

She says nothing, does nothing and still feels nothing. The pain and sense of violation she should feel confuses her. She knows she should be feeling something, anything, but it just is not there. Above all, she thinks she should feel ashamed. Not of what happened really, but of the fact that she waited all this time for this moment to test something she had always known to be true -- she doesn't belong to that place. She doesn't belong to the world. All of the horrors people inflict on each other, the permanent damage they cause each other, emotionally and physically, it is alien to her.

Yes, she can feel sympathy for others, even rage, if this had happened to someone else. She is connected to people, despite her relatively solitary lifestyle. The problem is that, when she is submersed in the unpredictable lives most people lead, such as when she left on her vacation, she disconnects from herself.

When alone, Morrigan can reconnect and truly enjoy things like art and the aurora, but she can not enjoy the superficial company of most people. She can not understand the superficial needs of men like Eric, especially when they feel they have a right to take what they need from others. It is like looking at a puzzle whose pieces do not fit together. The scant few things she enjoys in life are drifting away from her, here in this world of dramatic nightmares, but especially in Finland. What a beautiful place and an ironic place to find out that you have no passion for life, no emotions of your own apart from fear, but of all the wrong things. She knows something is wrong, something has finally clicked for her, but it isn't enough. Something tells her that more is coming. The pieces of the puzzle are being forced together.

The Winged Man sits cradling Morrigan. A shudder passes through his body as he looks down into her blank, staring eyes. He clutches at her, knowing that everything depends on her. She doesn't even suspect it, but he knows that the changes can go well or horribly, depending on how well she takes it. As the pieces crash together in Morrigan's mind, a piece of him breaks away leaving pain, shame and frustration.

While the Winged Man struggles with his immense feelings, Morrigan continues to lay there, unfeeling, uncaring and only aware of her own perplexing inner dialogue. The Winged Man wrenches out his sorrow for her. The emotions that literally rip through him would have killed the man responsible for them. In fact, they will, but he will not feel them. He will only feel pain and fear.

Chapter 9

It could have been minutes, hours or even days.

Morrigan blinked her eyes open in the dark bathroom. The first thing she became aware of was that she was in the tub, which was empty of water. The second thing she realized was that she was extremely sore and cold. Perhaps sore was not the word for it, she was in serious pain. Every muscle in her midsections screamed as reached for the light switch. She hit the switch and recoiled from its immediate glare.

Morrigan blinked several times before assessing the situation further. She looked down at her body. Bruises? Why were there bruises? Dark, red, blue and brownish bruises dotted her waist and stomach. She looked over at the tub and saw blood where she had been lying. She knew from where the blood had run. Further investigation hinted that she would heal without a trip to the emergency room. She just had to get cleaned up.

The hot water of the shower washed over her skin for twenty minutes before she tried to tolerate a washcloth on her. The extent of the bruising became apparent with every rub of the soapy cloth over her skin. Jolts ran through her body as she scrubbed.

Morrigan wondered, had she blacked out and fell? She didn't think it looked like it. In fact, the bottle she brought into the bathroom was as full as it had been last night. She remembered crawling in to the tub, meaning to take a bath, but she remembered nothing else. She could only assume that she fell asleep the moment she got in the tub, but that did not explain the bruising.

Excruciating pain made rubbing a towel on her skin impossible. Wrapped in a towel, she sat on the floor waiting for her skin to dry. She thought about ordering room service, but remembered the sauna and believed that would feel wonderful at the moment. She was hungry and in need of some serious relaxation, which she would not get in the room, looking at that bed.

Dressing took a long time. When Morrigan was finished, she looked outside for Eric's truck before stepping out into the dawn. She had not bothered to check the time before she left and realized it was quite early by the position of the sun in sky. Morrigan hoped the restaurant was open because she was very much in need of a coffee and some protein.

A crowd of five or six people had gathered around a swimming hole. Morrigan came across them on her journey to find sustenance. She had not braved the hole yet and thought to herself that she would not be able to now.

The people were standing around outside of the hole, looking down, but they did not appear to be looking into the hole, but rather next to it. In the distance, the fast grumble of snowmobiles got closer and closer. Made curious by the shocked, hushed tones that were coming out of some of the crowd and the sobs that suddenly emitted from one, Morrigan hobbled slowly and painfully over to the group.

"Ma'am, you might not want to . . . " one man said, but he was a moment too late.

Bile rose into Morrigan's throat. On the ground, laying on his side, was Eric. He was completely naked and there was a red visceral hole where his penis had been the night before. Her own pain became more acute when she glanced at it. Sudden panic hit Morrigan when her eyes flitted up from his groin and she stumbled away to vomit in the wood line. "I'm sorry, ma'am. I tried to warn you." was the last thing she heard before her own retching drowned out everything else.

On Eric's stomach and waist, in nearly an identical area as her bruises were the words, "I WANT YOUR ASS TOO." in block letters.

As Morrigan half walked, half hobbled back to her igloo, the thoughts going through her mind consisted primarily of, "What the fuck was that? Why the fuck? How the fuck? What the fuck am I going to do? I need to go home. Holy shit. Holy shit." The words were still running through her mind as she opened the door to her igloo, slammed it and locked it behind her.

Morrigan spent another hour on the floor of the bathroom crying and vomiting. She knew this had something to do with her. Those were the words Eric had said to her before she had felt the pain and disconnected. Did she do this? Was she losing time and memories? Was she capable of something like that? To the last, she wasn't sure.

Morrigan had always suspected she might be insane. As if to prove her thoughts correct, she started having a violent panic attack. The vomiting was a symptom of the panic, but now she was shaking uncontrollably. Her limbs felt numb and the thoughts became more intrusive and frightening. Doc and Marty could have told Morrigan that she was incapable of something so horrible, but they were very far away and Morrigan was very alone.

It was hours before Morrigan felt able to do anything. The sun had risen completely in the sky and she could hear her fellow resort goers bustling about engaging in their normal vacation activities. She suspected that the area she had stumbled on this morning was blocked off and the travelers were safe from the gruesome knowledge that a man had been murdered and carved like a Halloween pumpkin while they slept only a short walk away. This made her wonder if they had caught who had done it yet or if they were still searching. She pushed the thought away. There had to have been something she missed. That could not have been her, though the knowledge that it was obviously connected to her still nagged. She imagined what would have happened if she had reported the incident before realizing what had taken place at the watering hole. Such thoughts were unnecessary, as Morrigan would never have confided in strangers, but she could not help but think negative thoughts.

Hunger intruded on the negativity. Morrigan was horridly empty. She needed to venture out of her igloo, whether she liked it or not. She didn't want to be suspicious and she definitely wanted room service to change her bedding for her. She wasn't going to be able to do it herself.

She had checked the bed earlier and did notice a small blood stain. Practical Morrigan left tampons on the shelf in the bathroom in plain sight. It was embarrassing and led in the wrong direction, but it was better than unexplained blood in a guest bedroom after a man, who was not a guest of the hotel, was found dead on the premises.

Her feet slowly worked through the snow to the restaurant. Vomiting had drained her of what little energy she had earlier. The trek seemed very long and she imagined turning back more than once. Determination won.

She reached the restaurant and while she was waiting to be seated, she discovered by the way the staff kept huddling up in the corner between waiting on people that they knew what had happened. She took a chance and sat at the end of the bar, near the galley doors.

"Would you like a menu?" Morrigan heard as she gingerly sat herself on the bar stool. Maybe that hadn't been such a good idea.

"That would be fantastic." she said without enthusiasm. The petite bartender picked up a menu from somewhere below the bar and handed it to Morrigan.

"Can I get you a drink while you wait?"

"Yes, a shot of Crown and a cranberry juice, please. It has been a rough morning." She had decided she was going to be honest about her little discovery at the swimming hole and hope that the staff opened up to her in exchange for gossip. She knew her staff would have.

Like a good bartender, the girl behind the bar interacted with Morrigan as she poured her drink. Morrigan leaned in conspiratorially and said in a very low voice, "I saw something really fucked up this morning." Curiosity and knowledge flashed in the woman's eyes. Morrigan knew instantly that the bartender knew what had happened.

"Really?'

"Yes, did you hear about anything strange today?"

"Yes." the bartender said. "I heard there was a murder and even saw some police coming and going. We're not supposed to say anything, though." she looked slightly guilty, but clearly curiosity had killed that cat.

"That's what I am talking about. I saw the body." A gasp. She slammed down the shot the bartender handed her and gestured for another. She felt the panic rising up as she prepared to discuss the incident, but she knew she had to do it.

"Oh my god! I heard it was pretty bad." the bartender's voice dropped another key, "This is disgusting and I don't know if it is just a rumor, but I heard they found his penis in his butt." Morrigan almost chuckled at the kind of childish way the women said it, but and then realized what the woman had just said. Her gorge rose and she chugged down her cranberry juice to fight it. Another bad choice. Her stomach was boiling.

"Can I please have some crackers or something while I wait for food and can you put in an order of whatever your best sandwich is for me?"

"Of course." The bartender swooped some sort of bread from a window at the end of the bar and placed it before Morrigan. They began talking again as she fiddled with the keys on the screen that would send Morrigan's order to the kitchen.

"I didn't notice that last bit." Morrigan proffered between bites of bread. "What I did see was pretty gruesome, though."

"I would imagine."

The girl was starting to look genuinely sad and scared. This wasn't supposed to happen in the idyllic resort. This also showed Morrigan that they didn't know who did it yet. "Damn," she thought.

"They found out who he is a few minutes ago. At least, that is what Sam told me. I can't remember what he said his name was, but he mentioned that they found the guy's truck rental and were able to find out who was driving it when they traced the name. Turns out that it was rented in his wife's name, so they had to go find out from her who was driving the car."

Wife. Another blow to the guts. Just sit here, Morrigan. Eat your food. Be a good girl and do not vomit in this restaurant. Calm. Calm. Calm.

"That's very sad." she managed.

"Yes."

It seemed the bartender was equally as ready to squash the conversation as Morrigan was.

Morrigan managed to sit there and eat, but her thoughts were turning to poison. A wife. Her scarred hands shook. He was that kind of hurtful. Did he have kids? That prick. Then she would think of his body, lying dead and her feelings would conflict. Goddamn it. She knew she had to stay until her vacation was up now. This was just getting worse and worse.

Things did not get better after her meal. A trip to the sauna gained her a fun one-on-one with Mrs. Red and Curly herself. Morrigan had done her best to distance herself from the woman and give off the aura of one who does not want to talk. She should have figured the nosy, talkative woman would ignore her body language.

"It is sin, you know."

Morrigan took her time replying. She even considered ignoring the woman.

"What is sin, precisely?"

"Murder. If they do not find whoever mutilated that poor young man, I will not fret. God will mete out the proper punishment."

A shiver ran up Morrigan's spine. "How did you know that about that? How did you know that I know?"

"Oh, that is hardly the point, but I saw him this morning. I also saw you."

Morrigan tensed. "Saw me?"

"Before they came to take the young man away. You had to go vomit in the trees."

Morrigan was repulsed by the wet, red smile that crossed the woman's face as she recounted the event.

"You were there, then. Well, I have to agree that it was horrible. Let's hope they find whoever did it."

"Yes, lets," the woman said as she wrapped a towel around her fat, sweating body and waddled out the door.

Morrigan didn't sleep that night. Or the next night or the next. She drew. She drew the Winged Man. She drew the dwarf, she even drew Monty in checks in a tank top in her locker room. She missed the scant few people who she had in her life. Without sleep, she had no one. She wanted to go home. She wanted to talk to Doc. She wanted to cook and stock and do inventory. She wanted to sleep most of all. She wanted to escape her fear, which now had a name -- doubt. She couldn't. She didn't fall asleep again until two days before she was due to fly home. She had had to purchase another sketch book in town just to keep herself occupied.

Chapter 10

Morrigan is flying over a vast nothingness. The only thing to guide her is an ominous purple lit sky above and craggy rock outcroppings that rise up from the nothingness below. She swoops around these outcroppings, failing to enjoy her flying nightmare.

As always, when she visits this place, she has the sense that if she goes down, she will find there is much more to the nothingness than the nothing it hints at, but she is disinterested right now. She is not curious as she had been in the past, going down and down, yet finding nothing to assuage her curiosity. This time, she is headed somewhere, but she does not know where yet. She has to find something and in turn find someone.

Not far from Morrigan is a rocky outcropping that contains a stone room. There are walls, but they do not reach the ceiling and they jut out at odd angles. It is not a design that any architect in the real world would come up with. It is impractical and creepy in the way it hides so much of the room while still leaving it open to the rest.

On the floor are great cushions, like something out of Arabian nights. Along one wall are three fiery openings similar to fireplaces but that are spewing fire from deep below the room rather than burning fuel placed in them. There is a large opening to the front like the yawning mouth of a cave. There are no stairs leading up to the opening on the outside, though a wide staircase leads down into the room. Beside the solid staircase, hidden in the shadows, sits the Winged Man.

If ever there was a tortured being, the Winged Man is it. He has spent the past few days angry that he had spent his anger so quickly. He has no outlet now. Even his work is being carried out elsewhere -- something that Morrigan will have to come to know soon. He is unbalanced and can not function the way he should. So he came here, to the flying place where snow globe shaped nightmares linger and where only the most angry, sad or afraid dwell in their sleep.

He was there for days waiting for nothing, making new nightmares appear in the depths below. They were pouring out of a chasm inside of him that was in excruciating pain. The monster that dwells inside that chasm is writhing in guilt, anger, sacrifice and longing. The Winged Man's beautiful face, terrible in the grip of these emotions, had poured ink black tears for days. The blackness inside him had manifested outwardly. His perfect ivory skin is now black. Deep below him, tentacles reached out of the darkness for the other aberrations within while he grappled with his despair. He made the creatures destroy the other creatures and landscapes that sprang out of him, only to build more in their place. Their size, ferocity and sheer nightmarishness had increased exponentially in the past two days. He was so wrapped up in his cycle of madness that he did not hear Morrigan land lightly at the top of the stairs.

She stands there for a moment, wondering if the movement out of the corner of her eye is just a shadow. Squinting into the darkness beside the staircase, she sees the shape of a man – a beautiful man with black wings and onyx skin. Her feet slowly work down the steps, her eyes never wandering from the now still figure. Halfway down the staircase, Morrigan stops and lies with her stomach against the cold stone and peers over the edge at the Winged Man.

Despite his transformation, she watches him closely, fascinated by this opportunity and relaxing for the first time in days. He is still quite beautiful, but in a dark way that Morrigan likes. She sighs with longing nearly equal to his, but not nearly as terrible.

The Winged Man hears a sigh from above and snaps his head up to see Morrigan's face hovering two feet above him. In a flash, he stands to his full height, spreads his wings and bellows loudly in her face. The sound is horrifying, like an earthquake, a volcanic eruption or the destruction of a star. He is expressing his pain to her and the sound is unbearable.

"Stop!" she commands. His chest heaves as the tension dissipates. In that visceral scream, he had told her how he felt. He is very angry at her recent absence. He is angry that he could not see her. He is angry that sleep had not cooperated for both of their sakes. He is mostly angry at himself for wallowing in self pity.

"Why are you acting like this?" Morrigan asks. "What happened to you?" The room changes and she is sitting on the ledge shelving in her igloo. On the bed is Eric, alive again. She is with him. It is the night she wishes she could forget. However, this is something she does not remember. Eric is furiously beating her with his fists. He has her rolled on her side so he can take his pleasure in hitting her while he rapes her. Morrigan is shocked to see her eyes completely blank.

"What is this?" she cries.

The room changes back.

"That was what we both missed that night. Your "absence" was a favor from a friend who knew what was happening. My absence is inexcusable, but I really didn't know, Morrigan." It was hard for him to choke out the words. His voice was hoarse, though still somehow perfect.

"That's what happened to me, not what happened to you. Why are you a different color?"

"I'm sorry!" he bellows and something very big roared up from the darkness. He roars back, but only briefly because Morrigan is looking at him sternly again.

"Don't be sorry. I made a stupid decision. I paid for it. We need to talk about something else, though."

His face falls, mortified. Morrigan can tell that he does not want to talk to her. He is obviously upset about what had happened to her and concerned, but his wings are ruffling as if he wants to fly away.

"Did you see more that night? I mean later, after I fell asleep. I need to know."

A resigned sigh issues from his perfect, and now perfectly black, lips. This time the room does not change, but rather a mist appears in his hands as he cups them in front of himself. In it, she can see Eric walking the path to the swimming hole. Beside him walks a man both familiar and unfamiliar. A man who should be sporting wings, but is not.

The two men are talking as if they are pals. Morrigan cannot hear what they are saying, but it is clear that Eric is being led to the swimming hole. Once they reach it, the beautiful man raises the lid, exposing the icy water below, lifts Eric by the throat with one arm and throws him in. He closes the lid for a moment then lifts it again, pulling Eric out of the water. He begins shouting in Eric's face and Eric begins to strip. He does so slowly, pleading with his attacker as he does so, but there is no quarter coming from the currently wingless Winged Man.

As soon as Eric is naked, the Winged Man seizes Eric's neck with his arm and bends him backward so his stomach is stretched and exposed. A single talon bursts forth from the first finger of the Winged Man's right hand and he shows it to Eric, who screams. The talon shreds the words that are now familiar to Morrigan on Eric's skin then releases him. Eric looks down in complete shock, vomits and faints. The beautiful man rouses him with a kick to the groin. He makes Eric watch as he finishes the job and walks away, leaving Eric to bleed and freeze to death.

As the vision clears from the mist, the Winged Man looks across at Morrigan with pleading in his eyes. "Understand this" his eyes say. She can't, though, at least not completely. She hates what he has done, but can't bring herself to hate him.

"You were there?"

"Only after you fell asleep."

"Why haven't I ever seen you?"

"That is very complicated, but to be simple, I'm not allowed to yet."

"Allowed to? This is fucking absurd. I'm having a nightmare about a man in a dream coming through in real life and killing a man who attacked me, but you're telling me that you are not allowed to let me see you there? I just want to stay here."

"You can't. You can only have "sleepovers."" He smiles, though it is a reluctant grimace more than anything else.

She almost asks why he hasn't defied whatever is keeping them apart, but takes heed of his pain and remembers him saying he had not known. Instead of asking more questions and feeding the fuel of her disbelief, she changes the subject.

"What happened to you? You still haven't told me."

He shrugs, coming out of his fit easily. "Myself and those like me are prone to fits of temper and emotion. We rage, we have petty squabbles. We are driven by emotion. I felt a particularly keen one and it transformed me." he looks down at himself and seems embarrassed, "Don't worry." he adds quickly "I will not be this way for long."

"I wasn't worried." she says, "You are always perfect looking. Isn't that how I made you?" she winks at him

"I told you, Morrigan" he replies, unwilling to joke around, "You didn't make me. I have parents and two brothers. You didn't make them, either."

Morrigan is getting tired of trying to figure out why her nightmares are so fucking strange. She is used to the long conversations that shouldn't make sense, the landscapes that should be dreamy, but are clear as day, etc. She doesn't want to bother with this cryptic back and forth right now. She has been stuck in the stark reality of Finland dealing with the most terrifying crisis of her life alone, though the alone part isn't the problem. She is used to that. It is just that she is more comfortable here. She wants to relax. She wants something other than the loneliness that had invaded her every moment since Eric. She also wants to enjoy the freedom that she feels here from the pain inflicted by him. She can't feel the wounds. She can also be with the creature before her, where she wants to be, if she can only stay here.

Morrigan reaches for him, holds his head in her hands and pulls it toward her breast. She hugs him there for a moment, soothing the impossibly tall and bent over man before her. He is amazed. No one has ever comforted him this way in all of his years -- which are too many to mention. The piece inside him is still broken by the events of the past week, but something else is happening as well. Something is settling into place that he knows would never go away, but he has known it would happen. Morrigan leaves a kiss on his curly hair and releases his head from her grasp.

"Morrigan, I want to show you something, but I think you will wake too soon for me to do it tonight. I'm to take you away from your nightmares for one night and show you something that no one like you has ever seen before. Do you remember the house we went to together, not the nightmarish one?" She nodded and they both smiled, remembering what had happened. "I will meet you there when you come back to me." he kisses her and she wakes up.

Chapter 11

Morrigan's last hours in Finland were uneventful. She managed to avoid talking about the Eric incident, but also avoided sleeping, to her disappointment. The aurora still comforted her at night, but there was nothing left in the wintery landscape to hold her there. She was eager to get home and return to the restaurant and her otherwise stark life.

She flew home and spent her first few hours in her apartment sitting on the couch in the dark. She thought about going to the restaurant to check in, but Monty didn't expect her back until the next day. She didn't have any messages on her machine, so she assumed that she could spend the last night of her vacation collecting her thoughts or more like purging her brain of the events that had occurred during her vacation.

After she was sure she was not on the verge of some mental breakdown preceded by a bout of extreme calm in the face of this unusual situation, Morrigan got up off the couch and wandered into the kitchen. Flipping on the light switch, she remembered that she didn't have anything worth eating in the house. She had rid the premises of all perishable items before leaving the country. Instead of opening a can of something she was sure she wouldn't enjoy, she decided to go to the local deli on the corner. A sandwich sure beat a can of ravioli she had purchased in a moment of idiocy.

It wasn't as cold here as Morrigan had been for the past two weeks, but she still needed her jacket. She grabbed it as she walked out of the apartment, clicking the lock into place as she went. The deli was at the corner only a few minutes away, so she didn't have far to go. As she walked, her focus turned to the days ahead. She had an appointment with Dr. Bateson and work to do at the restaurant. These mundane, normal thoughts kept her as her feet found their way to food.

The bright lighting of the deli brought Morrigan back to the moment and the task at hand. She ordered a chicken, greens and avocado wrap, then grabbed a bag of chips and a water before sitting at the table nearest the deli window. Looking out into the night, she let her eyes wander to the intersection outside the window. Her heart began fluttering. This was the intersection where she last saw the dwarf and Doomsey. When her eyes alit on them, she noticed a third figure standing there.

This third figure was naturally taller than the dwarf, but surprisingly still much taller than Doomsey. She squinted through the glass to catch this other figure, imagining in the back of her mind that it was a police officer giving the men, she thought the term in regard to the dwarf man rather loosely, a hard time. She heard the worker behind the counter call out her ticket number and removed her attention from the window. Forgetting the odd sight for a moment, she retrieved her sandwich and put her chips and drink in the bag with it.

The bell above the door jingled as she walked out of the shop. Returning curiosity caused her to turn and look across the intersection at Doomsey and his growing entourage. A passing car blocked her view long enough that she made it several more steps away before actually getting a good look at the group. The third man was crossing the street quickly in her direction. She recognized his face instantly and nearly dropped her dinner. It was Eric, whose surname she had never devised.

His clothes were in tatters and he had a short, scruffy beard that was not there when she first met him. His hair was slightly longer and unkempt, but none of these details kept Morrigan's attention for very long. It was his face that drew her. His face was marked by something that she could not put her finger on. She was already walking quickly away from the corner, her eyes meeting his and his glaring back when she recognized it for what it was -- sheer madness.

Finally afraid again and sadly removed from what she thought was going to be a calm night, Morrigan ran to her apartment. She was up the stairs and in her apartment with the door locked before she could think. She was on the verge of panic again. Short, incoherent sentences littered her thoughts. "How the . . .? Did I imagine . . . ? Is this real . . . .? Is it him . . .?"

Then, it finally clicked into place that an undead man who was murdered by an apparition in her nightmares after he had raped her had just chased her home from the corner. In spite of her rapidly beating heart and shaking limbs, she made it over to the window after ascertaining that there were no noises coming from the other side of her door.

Her curtains rustled as she moved them aside, nearly closing her eyes as she did so to prevent herself from seeing the figure that might be standing outside. The heavy curtains did not slide aside easily. She had to curl her fingers around the edge near the middle and pull them from the top to prevent them from catching on the rod and bringing the whole contraption down too soon for her comfort. She chastised herself for not purchasing sturdier rods when she moved in. Not being a "Let the sun shine in" kind of person, she assumed she would never move them.

She could feel the thick threads of her expensive curtains snagging on the burred edge of her cheap, landlord installed curtain rod. She only needed an inch to see out of the window, but sweeping them across instead of moving the whole curtain on the rod was bound to shift the weight and take it down, which would leave her feeling unbearably exposed. So, she tugged a little as it snagged, hoping it would come free without issue. After what felt like ten minutes of listening to the delicate pops and subtle hisses of fabric in distress, she had moved the curtain enough so that she could look out.

There he was, outside her window. Not on the street below and not standing on the fire escape balcony that was one floor below her -- the ladder and balcony to her floor had long ago fallen off the side of the building. How the fuck was his face right in front of hers? She didn't dare to look away to check, though his torso must have been visible in the window from this height. She was afraid because she knew he must be hovering there and therefore, she was completely fucking nuts.

His eyes found hers and she swore she could hear something between a guttural laugh and a growl emit from his dirty, slobbering mouth. The face of this monster whom she had thought dead hovered not an inch from the glass, as close as hers was on the other side of the window. It was no longer attractive. There was something deranged and wild about it.

Before Morrigan could do anything that the rational part of her brain told her to do, such as close the curtain, run, scream, faint or call the police, the Eric face began licking the glass like a hot canine would lick ice cream his master put in his bowl on a hot day. His hands pressed against the glass on either side of his face, the nails scratching and leaving jagged stripes in the city grime that clung to the outside of the windows.

This disgusting display caused her to react. Despite her utter fear, she pulled herself back from the window by a foot. Her movement caused the curtain to close slightly, leaving a smaller gap for the two foes to gauge each other through. The movement made the Eric creatures eyes to open wide and his head to move so his face was centered in the new gap. Morrigan noticed that his movements were jerky and stilted, as if there was a strobe light directed at him that no one could see and that only affected him.

With eyes still wide open and tongue still repeatedly pressing against the glass, the Eric thing rapped on the window with a single open palm. In between raps, he scratched with the nail on his right index finger. Within seconds, he was pounding on the glass with both hands and had moved his head back, flipping his tongue in and out rapidly, but no longer close enough to touch the window. Finally, his head came forward in a flash and smashed against the glass.

Morrigan racked her brain for something to do. Confronting the thing would only cause her to throw herself out the window and injure herself, especially if he was just a figment of her imagination. She also couldn't contact anyone because her first order of business is to hide the fact that she is seeing things until she can get to the doctor. On the other hand, if she isn't nuts, confronting Eric might get her killed. It would also mean that he is back from the dead, trying to get at her, perhaps for revenge. He had failed to kill her with his relentless beating the last time. Perhaps he was back to succeed. She might have had a fighting chance if he were human, but she had no idea what he was now -- human, zombie, apparition. She didn't want to risk it, so confrontation was out.

She could run to her bedroom and hope that the heavy door between her bedroom and living room would be enough to keep out the undead thing, but that was out of the question too. She had no idea how it was maintaining its position outside of that window. There was nowhere for it to stand and no way for it to have climbed up. That meant it could feasibly and inexplicably make its way over to the bedroom window, despite the idea being near impossible. There, she could lock herself in the bathroom, but that gave her no egress.

Her only other option was to flee the apartment building. She could run down the stairs and out the front door, hoping that help was out there. A conveniently placed police car or a kind pedestrian might be enough. However, he had seen her go in that door, had presumably seen the movement in her living room window and scaled the wall. If there was no help to be had out there, which was quite possible, he would be on her in seconds. She could go out the back, though. He had not seen that entrance and may not know it was there, unless he had been casing her apartment building.

All of these thoughts went through Morrigan's head in a matter of seconds. When she was done mapping out her plan, she realized that she was still holding her takeout food. She dropped the bag and ran to the door. She heard nothing behind her until she flipped the deadbolt and opened the door. The sound of violently breaking glass followed her into the hallway. She slammed her door shut as she ran. If she could get around the corner fast enough, he would not know which way she had gone. She whipped around the corner, running for the backstairs at the far end of the hall. She made for them as fast as she could, the muscles in her torso screaming with the exertion and the effect the stretching muscles had on her injuries.

Not bothering to listen, but still hearing the door to her apartment slam open against the hallway wall, Morrigan kept her eyes forward and pushed her battered body as hard as it would go. She reached the stairs and jumped down them three steps at a time and out the back door. Without pausing, she took a left through the alleyway that would spell her death if Eric caught on to her and caught up with her. She didn't let that thought slow her down.

A right down another alley and a brief run up the street brought her to the dock door at Morrigan's. Her keys were in her pocket from when she first entered her apartment. On the key ring was a key for the restaurant's dock door, but she didn't have the time or patience to use it. She pressed the bell and held it. Monty opened the door the kitchen wide, looking like he was about to yell at whoever was ringing his bell. Instead, he looked quickly at Morrigan and then past her.

"Hey! This isn't public property. Fuck off." As he said it, he noticed that there was something wrong with the man who lurked in the shadows behind his boss. Morrigan still did not look, though she had a good idea what was happening and how close she had come to not having the help she had desperately needed. Monty grabbed her arm and pulled her through the door, something he normally wouldn't have dared to do. She had been right. He had to be seeing the Eric thing behind her.

She turned as her feet made purchase in the kitchen, next to a uniform-clad Monty. There, not ten feet away, an oddly staring, drooling Eric shifted back and forth on his feet and cocked his head first to the right, then to the left. To Morrigan, he looked like a predator getting ready to pounce. Confirming this image, he stuck the tip of his tongue out of the outer edge of his mouth and made a slurping sound as he swept it across his bottom lip.

"You're not deaf, so you must be insane. I said to get the fuck out of here, jackass. I'm not going to call the police until after I'm done kicking the shit out of you."

The rasping, guttural laugh groan came from Eric again and he stepped forward. During this time, Morrigan had not been standing there idle. She had been assessing the situation. This time, her best plan did not match Monty's. She grabbed his arm and yanked him back as hard as she could, swinging the door shut just as the predatory rapist zombie leapt through the air toward them. Morrigan had no need to deadbolt it or run. It was a steel entry door that closed and locked without much help from anyone. She figured the steel would hold him and was satisfied to hear a thump against the door and see no give from either the door or the frame.

She wondered if the undead were polite and didn't crash parties because she was almost certain she had a restaurant full of guests and employees out front and a kitchen full of chefs and dishwashers out back. Right now wasn't the time to decide what the hell was going on here. If Monty can see it, that is enough to know that she and everyone between her and it were in big trouble. She was finally experiencing what a nightmare would feel like from the perspective of someone who is frightened by them. The panic attack was coming, but it could wait.

"Holy shit, Morrigan. Are you okay?" Monty looked extremely concerned, but did not appear to be freaking out as one would if they realized that was some supernatural entity chasing Morrigan.

"I think so. We should go check out front to make sure he isn't coming around."

"He isn't coming around."

Thump, thump, thump. Monty was right. He was still at the back door.

"I'm going to call the cops."

Morrigan did not object to contacting the authorities. Really, there was no risk to herself. If the man said he was a rapist that met Morrigan in Finland, was subsequently murdered by a tall guy with a very sharp claw and then rose from the dead to chase Morrigan, chances were, Morrigan wasn't the one getting locked up for being insane.

There was an office phone hanging on the wall around the corner from where Monty and Morrigan stood. Instead of leaving Morrigan where she stood and calling the police. He grabbed her hand, pulled her with him and was dialing 911 before he let go. As he spoke to the operator on the other end -- saying something about a homeless guy chasing his boss into Morrigan's -- she said, "I'm going to check out front."

The thumping had stopped and only she had noticed it. He rolled his eyes and she walked through the kitchen toward the front of the house. Monty was behind her within 30 seconds and stood with her at the front window staring into the night. She didn't see anything out of the ordinary, nor did Monty. She said nothing to any of the rest of the staff, as she didn't want to scare anyone and was still wrapping her mind around the problem.

"Let's meet the police out front, so we don't have any problems."

Monty scoffed. "Why don't we wait in front of the door and then go out when

the cops get here?"
The night bartender -- Rob -- was already looking at the two of them as if he knew something was going on, but he was unlikely to give a shit, so Morrigan agreed with Monty. They would wait inside the door.

"Mind telling me what happened?"

Morrigan paused for a moment. What should she tell him? Did she want the police to know the chase had started at her apartment? After a brief moment of thought, she realized there was absolutely nothing about the attack that would connect her and him to Finland. She was on the guest list in Finland, but he was definitely on the dead list there, so what harm could reporting this do? It didn't really matter if she didn't report it, either, though, because she sure as fuck wasn't going back to her apartment.

Her hesitation wasn't missed by Monty. "Hey, if you want to keep it to yourself, whatever."

"Nah, it's okay. I was just wrapping my head around what happened." she decided to mix up the story a bit, as it wouldn't suit to describe why she had been running from him in the first place, so she started in her apartment. "I was sitting in my living room getting ready to eat a sandwich from that deli on the corner." Monty winced. "Shut up. I had just got home. At any rate, fucker, I heard something against my window, thought maybe my curtain was jacked up or something, went to check and that goon was staring at me through the window."

"How the fuck?"

"I think he propped a ladder on the escape or something." She didn't bother to mention that he did not look like he was on a ladder at all.

"Go on." He was looking at her intently now, clearly happy she was okay, but concerned that she had gone through so much. Morrigan really liked Monty for that. She hadn't realized how much she wanted to not be alone in this. Her nightmare boyfriend of sorts didn't count when she was stuck here in the real world.

"Well, I backed away from the window and before I knew it . . . " leaving out the licking weirdness for now ". . . he had smashed the window with something and I was running like hell out of the back door and to here."

"Well, thanks for bringing him to me." Monty said sarcastically, but with a clear note of relief that she had made it here. "You know, Morri, that fuck was right behind you. I don't want to freak you out or anything, but next time, you might want to stick to the crowded streets."

She didn't bother telling him that the Eric thing might have had help from a demented dwarf obsessed with screams, had she taken that route. She didn't want to freak him out; i.e. make him think she was insane. Besides, the police had arrived. They pushed through the glass front doors, holding them open for a diner walking in as they walked out.

An officer emerged from the passenger side of a cruiser parked at the curb in front of Morrigan's. His partner shut down the vehicle and emerged from the driver's side. "Hello, officers." Monty said in his most polite because I have to be voice.

The tall middle-aged and mustached police officer regarded Monty with a look that said, "I know you from somewhere and, if I don't, I sure as hell know your type." Morrigan laughed a little on the inside. She figured there was an illegal substance somewhere in her restaurant or on Monty that, either way, belonged to Monty.

"Did you call 911?"

"Yes, I did."

"Where is the man you called about?"

The officer and his partner looked more alert now. The first man kept his eyes on Monty, awaiting an answer, while the other scanned the area silently.

"The last we heard him, he was out back behind the restaurant. He was pounding on the dock door to be let in."

Something passed between the officers wordlessly and the first officer walked off around the parking lot of the building, obviously intending to circle around the back. The second officer, who was roughly the same age and build of the first came to stand in front of Morrigan and Monty. He pulled a notebook from the front pocket of his uniform and began asking questions. He gave the standard, "What happened?" and Morrigan gave him the same answer she had given Monty, though the end of the story was told mostly by Monty, who had seen the guy more clearly.

Morrigan lied and said she could say nothing of the man's build, given that she had only seen his face through the window and had not seen him clearly after Monty pulled her into the restaurant. This got her an odd look from Monty that went unnoticed by the officer. Monty knew damn well that she turned all the way around in that doorway to get a look at the guy, but she was damned if she was going to describe a man who had just died in a hotel in Finland where she was staying to the police. She would rather not have a complicated lie, either. She simply didn't see his build clearly. His face was nondescript. Too dark to tell his eye color, dark hair ,square jaw and that is all she wrote.

The officer who had gone around back came to the front while the second officer was still asking questions. He let his partner finish up by asking Morrigan the address to her apartment and asking for permission to search the premises. She handed him the key in her pocket and gave him the address. She figured he wouldn't need the key, but also figured he would lock her apartment after he left. She wondered if any of her less than stellar neighbors had gotten to her stuff yet and figured they probably had. Fuck. Luckily, she had everything important on the computer at work and had left her laptop here with Monty, so he could put in orders from home after doing inventory at night. He probably didn't, but she had wanted to go easy on him.

The first officer began speaking as soon as the second was finished taking down Morrigan's address.

"It looks like Mr. Wonderful took off, but he did some pretty extensive damage to your door. I assume he hit it with something before taking off. I have officers searching the area for him and we will be checking up here and at your home tonight, though you probably want to stay with a friend tonight, Ms. Fuseli. We're going to go do our jobs. We suggest you leave the restaurant in groups tonight and keep the back door locked. You'll need to get it replaced tomorrow."

Replaced? That got another patented weird look from Monty. What the hell had the two of them missed? They went back into the restaurant and headed toward the back door where there were three cooks and a dishwasher staring at the dock door. It was mangled and pushed in on the entire lower half. An arm could fit between the gap in the door and the door frame.

"Fuck."

Morrigan was getting irritated with her luck. She and Monty stood around assuring the cooks and exchanging surprised comments about what had happened for about ten minutes before ordering the cooks back to work. It was enough to amuse them for a bit, but in a trade where things regularly caught on fire and trips to the hospital were not uncommon, they were over it in an hour. Morrigan and Monty on the other hand were not convinced of anything.

"Perceptive little shit." Morrigan thought when Monty pointed at the door and said, "That doesn't make any sense."

Neither of them was willing to step outside to prove their theory, but both were relatively certain that there was nothing out there to grab and the Eric thing had not had enough time between standing there slobbering and the door closing in his face to grab anything from outside of the back dock area. He had slammed against the door the moment they closed it and had thumped away every few seconds for about half a minute before he stopped. The only explanation left was that the guy was a brick shithouse. Morrigan didn't add to the conversation that she thought he could hover too.

"Shall I call a door guy?"

"I would think so. Tell him to be here as early tomorrow as he can."

"You got it, chef."

Monty went into the office to make the call. Morrigan was about to make a remark about him using the wall phone, but then remembered that he had probably gotten pretty used to her office in the past two weeks. "Let it be." she thought. "Perhaps it is time for me to have a partner." The thought surprised her, but fit right. Monty as a partner in Morrigan's? The little shit had no money. He would have to pay her off his profits and bust his ass, probably living in the office for the next few years, but he could do it. She stored it away for later perusal and moved away from the door. It was creeping her out something fierce.

Morrigan finally got a chance to eat and then hopped on line for a few hours to soothe her nerves while Monty handled the door guy and whatever nonsense the front of the house brought back for her to deal with. She could get used to having Monty running the ship with her. After closing, most of the staff welcomed her back and took off. It was only her and Monty left in the restaurant when they decided to leave. Morrigan had not given a single thought to where she would stay that night. She was definitely going to the station tomorrow to get her keys, but more than that, she had no idea.

"So, you're crashing at my place, right?' Monty asked as they stepped out in the night. "Because you sure as fuck are not walking back down that street by yourself."

"I don't know. I hadn't thought about it."

"Well I did." Without saying another word about it, they entered the parking lot and went to get into his car before he paused. "Morri, this might sound weird, but I want to check out that door from the back."

She sucked in her breath. "You sure, man? That does sound weird."

"Yeah, I'm sure. The pigs said they would be scoping the place out all night. I saw one drive by when we walked out."

She knew she was being suckered into something stupid, but she was getting curious herself. "All right. Let's check it out, but pull your car around back first so we can hop back in it if the shit hits the fan." Monty agreed.

As it turned out, they didn't have to get out of the car to see what had been done. Not only was the door caved in, there were scratches all over it. When had those scratches gotten there? Neither she or Monty had heard any scratching, just pounding. It dawned on her as she stared at them. "Get the fuck out of here, Monty." He was already in drive and slammed on the gas, tearing around the other side of the building and out into the street. They both knew it without saying it. Those scratches had to be new. There was no way they were made when the two of them were standing there and the officer had said nothing about them.

On top of Morrigan's, a figure crouched near the edge of the roof, watching the white sedan peel down the street. It slurped, jumped off the roof and slinked off into the night.

Chapter 12

Morrigan and Monty sat on the couch in his small apartment. Monty had a lot of questions that Morrigan did not want to answer, so she directed the conversation to the health of the restaurant in her absence.

"How did things go?"

"Fine. I really do think we need a new bread guy, though. I mean, we do crazy, but that guy is in everyone's way." He walked off into the attached kitchen with the two empty beer bottles that sat on the coffee table.

"I agree." she said, as he grabbed two more beers, without needing to ask her if she needed another one.

"Listen, I have no idea if you have any idea what that was all about and I understand if you don't want to talk about." He paused as he plopped back onto the couch and handed her a bottle. "I just have to say that you and I both know that was not normal. I would be scared shitless, if I were you, whether I knew what that was about or not."

She shrugged and he continued.

"I really want to know is if that was some weird freakish random thing we will probably never see again or if that was some freakish thing that is out to get you in particular. I think you know which it is."

She didn't bother to protest. "I'd say the latter."

"Then what do we do?"

"*We* don't do anything, Monty. I doubt there is anything either of us could do anyway, but I think I am going to need to take a longer hiatus from the restaurant and give you a raise, probably a substantial one."

"I don't mind keeping up with the restaurant while you're gone. You don't need to give me a raise. The extra hours more than make up for it, but what are you going to do in the meantime?"

"Hear me out. I'm not talking about a raise in the typical meaning of the word. I am talking about selling you half of the restaurant and, therefore, leaving you with half of the profits. In a way, it is actually a pay cut that will pay off more in the long run."

He exhaled sharply, ran one hand through his hair and sank back into the couch. "I'm flattered, but I think we'll just pretend you didn't say that until a better time."

"No, Monty. If you want half of Morrigan's, it is yours. We can even change the name, but Morrigan comes before Monty."

He laughed, "What else is new?"

"Now that hurt my feelings, you dick."

"What do we do in the meantime? I just pretend you're on a longer vacation, run the restaurant and hope you come back someday in one piece?"

"Not quite. I'll be around while I'm on hiatus. I will have to collect what I need to live and you will still have to run major changes by me until we have a system."

"All right. I'm in."

She punched him on the arm. "Awesome. Now you should go to bed. You have deliveries in the morning and I have a meeting I definitely cannot miss."

Monty sighed and stood up without saying another word. He retrieved some blankets and pillows for her from a hall closet, downed the rest of his beer and slunk off to his room.

She spend the rest of the night laying on his couch, staring at the ceiling and listening for noises at the window.

Morrigan sat in the waiting room for twenty minutes while the doc finished up with another patient. Just as it was uncharacteristic of her to be late, it was the same for her being early. She simply had nothing else to do and was unwilling to go home to retrieve anything, as she would have to pass the three nightmareteers or risk being late for her appointment.

By the time the doc was finished, she was bored and stressed out, which she had managed to avoid being for most of the awkward morning she had spent talking to Monty and pretending the biggest thing going on was him getting half of the restaurant. She could take the pay cut with ease. Most of what she had made since the restaurant opened had gone into savings.

"Ms. Fuseli, he's waiting for you." said the middle-aged and unattractive, but polite to a fault, women behind the reception desk. Morrigan smiled and thanked her before opening the door to Doc's office.

He looked up from his desk and acknowledged her entrance with a nod. She sat in her usual spot and watched him walk over to his.

"Hello, Morrigan. It's good to see you are back."

She nodded. His brows pressed together at her lack of response.

"I trust your vacation went well."

"I'm not so sure I would say that."

"Did something specifically go wrong while you were away?"

She lied and covered it up with a half-truth. "No. It was just longer than I needed and I had a break-in last night when I came home."

"*When* you came home?"

"Yes, I was in the apartment. The man chased me to the restaurant." She figured telling him that much would convey at least part of her problem to him.

"Wow, Morrigan. Did he try to hurt you?"

"I think that was the idea."

"That is a lot of stress you just got put under. How do you feel?"

"Scared. More scared than I have ever been." She was being completely honest now.

"That is natural. After all that you have been going through and now to be faced with this? I am not at all surprised that you are experiencing a setback right when you could have been making a little progress."

"The first few nights I was in Finland, I really did feel like I had found a way to balance everything. Now, I just feel like a useless bag of nerves. I can't explain anything; I can't predict anything. I have no idea what is going on and it makes me extremely uncomfortable."

"Morrigan, not being able to predict everything is a part of life. What you have to do is perhaps not really understand that so much as learn to cope with it. You have to face what is unpredictable and develop a sort of predictable response to it -- one that you are comfortable with. Of course, discussing that can be a back burner issue. I think it is pertinent that we deal with this crisis in your life. Did the police catch the man that was chasing you?"

"No."

"What is going through your mind about that?"

"He knows where I live and he knows where I work. He didn't try to steal anything in the apartment (she knew he wasn't interested in that, but decided to let Tynan think that she had no idea who this man was). I assume he was there to hurt me."

"That sounds reasonable, Morrigan. Frightening, but a reasonable assumption."

She knew he wanted her to elaborate, as he paused and said nothing more. She obliged. "I know you are wanting to know how I feel about that. The truth is, I feel like he could come back. I am staying at Monty's, or at least, I did last night. I have taken another vacation from work in an effort to keep the restaurant free from whoever this guy is until the police can catch him."

Again, she was adding some normal responses to her honest responses to make the situation seem less paranormal than she believed it was. Until Monty had answered the door last night, Morrigan was convinced she really was going insane. Despite all of the rationalizations she had come up with before then, she had still sensed a loss of grip on reality. More and more, she had been denying that any of this could be real and simply assuming she was losing her shit. When Monty saw the Eric thing for something more than just a violent man, she had known something about her nightmare life had leaked out or that her "real" life was closer to her nightmare life than she had previously imagined.

"Again, a rational manner of handling things, though I should think that the restaurant is still relatively safe. There are many people there. Your apartment, however, given that you live alone, may be best visited with company in the interim. At any rate, what is important is that we deal with your emotions. You have always been quite able to handle the rest."

Tynan Bateson leaned toward Morrigan. It was the closest he ever came to being personal with her. He was professional to a fault, but his small mannerisms, such as the leaning toward Morrigan, made her feel safe, like she was with someone whose concern was genuine. It made her feel a little better now.

"I don't know. I want to 'deal' with my emotions. I'm afraid that talking about them will make them worse"

"And that stems from . . . ?"

She paused to think about that open statement for a moment. What were the basics of her fear? Of course, vacation rapist comes back from the dead after being brutally murdered by nightmare companion to hunt her down and do something horrible to her again seemed to suit the situation, but Morrigan was not really afraid of what the man would do to her. It was what he represented that scared the shit out of her.

"That I cannot predict that situation. More so, that I am losing my mind."

"Where does the fear you are losing your mind stem from?"

She started to get frustrated. It wasn't Doc's fault that she was afraid to "share" what was going on, but his questions hit too close. He always knew when something different popped up. Any chink she left in her armor was easily exploited by the Doc. She heaved a sigh and put her face in her hands. Her sweater came down over her palms, so her face warmed fast as the fabric soaked up the heat from her breath. The condensation did little to mask the fact that tears were now seeping from her eyes.

The Doc sat patiently, watching her, resisting the all too human urge to comfort her physically with a pat on the back or a hug. When she was done grappling with her embarrassment, she lifted her face to him. He saw absolute turmoil reflected back in her eyes. She was definitely in need of reassurances, but he had few to give her. He knew she was holding out on him, that she wouldn't respond to pressure and that the only thing she would ever accept from him was someone to talk to. Every little triumph Morrigan had in the area of her terrors, anxiety and nightmares, though few, were of her own doing. She treated herself. Doc was a sounding board. She resisted every type of treatment he suggested. Morrigan was simply a person who did nothing she didn't think of herself. The vacation had been a small victory for the Doc, but it was something she always wanted to do. It took him the better part of a year to get her to do it. He didn't have that long to implement another of her ideas in a way that she would use it. He decided to be frank.

"Morrigan, there is nothing I can do to make you feel better if you are not willing to compromise. I really want to help you. I want you to bounce back from this feeling, if not better than before, at least not as bad as you feel now. Your anxiety, from what I can tell, is at the low end, as in not an attack, but it is constant at the moment. It is going to wear away at you until something gives. I hope that it is the police catching this guy or you catching a break, but it could be you that gives, not the rest of the world."

"You could be right." his eyes looked briefly sad at her response, but they continued their session without another hitch. They reiterated how she could take control of her anxiety as it happened and he stressed the utmost need for her to get enough rest. He knew sleep helped her relieve stress, just like anyone else, but he also had the sense that sleep was the key to all of her problems or, more accurately, the content of her sleeping thoughts. He ended the session by scheduling another for two days hence. He also insisted that she call him should anything come up. She said she would, smiled and left, not quite sure where she would go next.

~~~~~~~~~~

A 'normal" person, thought Morrigan, would call their parents or a close approximation. Morrigan had none. She might have called her long lost best friend, but really, she had no idea what to say. Monty, the weirdest, most competent and down to earth person she knew was busy keeping her life's work together while she had a mental breakdown. She had no one to talk to. She decided to get her truck, trio of psychos be damned, eat at the restaurant and then come up with some sleeping arrangement that would actually end in sleep for her. Besides, she needed her clothes too and her suitcase and travel toiletries were still in the truck.

It took Morrigan a half an hour to reach the intersection leading to her house. She could have gone around to avoid the nightmarish duo coupled with her favorite crazy homeless man, but she was in no mood to walk farther and curiosity drove her to push the inevitable. She was a little surprised to see all three of them there, though. Something inside her had just assumed that the Eric thing would take the human route and hide from the police. He had, in a way. He hid in plain sight.

Morrigan mustered the last strand of confidence that she had left and marched toward the intersection. As she approached, she saw that only the dwarf man and the Eric thing were leering at her. Doomsey looked taxed. He avoided looking up and had lost his habit of shouting at everyone who gave him the opportunity. That was interesting to Morrigan, but not surprising. She had no idea what was passing between the three of them, but assumed it was uncomfortable. She wondered how long Doomsey would last before the dwarf man drove him to suicide or the Eric thing tore him into little pieces.

She was so mentally exhausted that she went a little insane herself. She stopped on the other side of the street from the trio, stared right back at them and flipped the Eric thing her middle finger. She even mouthed "Fuck you" at him. Morrigan didn't expect this to do much in the way of deterring the monster, but she certainly didn't expect what actually happened. In hindsight, she should have.

The Eric thing got noticeably excited. It began rocking back and forth on its heels and drooling even more than it had been. How did no one notice the copious amounts of fluid leaking from this man's face? The truth was that people were averting their eyes unconsciously. They noticed something was wrong about this man. Trying desperately not to show the fear that had welled up inside of her, Morrigan simply started walking toward her truck again. Much to her surprise, only his eyes followed her. The dwarf began banging things again, seemingly becoming bored with her torment, now that it was clear she was afraid.

Her truck was parked less than a block away. She hopped in the second she got to it, started it and took off without bothering to let it warm up. She drove by the objects of her torment again, pausing for a second to reiterate the fact that she thought they should fuck off. The Eric thing was no longer there. She looked around while trying to pay attention to where she was going. She didn't see him anywhere. Giving in finally, she retrieved her cell phone from her pocket and dialed the Doc's number.

Forty-five minutes later, Morrigan was standing in a line at the pharmacy up the street from Monty's apartment. She had called him and asked if it was cool for her to try to crash out on his couch. He implied that he thought it was a given that she was staying there, hence the key he had left her when he went to work. He told her to stay safe and that he would be home after closing. If Morrigan could get back to his house and to sleep within the next hour, that would give her eight hours of sleep and eight hours away from the horror that had become her life.

Back at the apartment, she set up her bed on the couch, retrieved her laptop from Monty's room and logged onto a movie website. She went to the kitchen for a beer to wash down her pills and heated the soup she had purchased at the pharmacy. While she waited, she brushed her teeth and changed into some clean pajamas from her suitcase. Within minutes, she was eating her soup and watching a historical drama about some monarch with a complicated train of mistresses and wives. She got about half way through the movie before she fell asleep.

~~~~~~~~~~

She is on a gilded terrace, standing before two huge gates, through which ephemeral wisps pass. Holding her hand is her only comfort. She turns toward him, feeling utter relief. His skin is a dark blue, not quite the black it had been when she last saw him. He looks down at her with matching relief in his eyes. A sob forces its way out of her center and she leans against his chest to let it out. He holds her head against himself and tries to absorb her pain, a power which he does not possess.

When Morrigan is done unraveling, she looks up at the Winged Man, who smiles down at her. Her face is absolutely beautiful covered in tears. She looks the same here as she does in life, but he sees her with eyes no mortal could ever see through. He sees the little tendrils of hair matted against her face and held in place by the moisture of her sweat and tears. He uses his hands to push them back from her face, kissing her softly on the lips as he does so. Morrigan is shocked into composure. She is never quite prepared for how it feels to be kissed by this confusing, depraved, sweet and completely mysterious creature she dreams of so often. He pulls his face away from hers.

"I wanted to take you somewhere, remember?" She nods. "We're here, Morrigan."

He grasps her waist and turns her away from the two imposing gates. She does a 180-degree turn and gasps. Before her is a snow globe unlike any she has been presented with. Within the boundaries of her globular sleep vision, there are breathtaking gardens containing flowers no one could classify. She knows without asking that they only exist here.

Among these gardens and waterfalls that she sees in her peripheral vision, there are three hovering castles. The one in the center is large, rosy marble, multi-terraced and contains more towers than she can count. She sees carved statues in every available space. Gargoyles, angels and shapes she does not recognize hide in every nook and cranny.

The castle on the left is grayish black. It is covered in slick looking black ivy. Where the center castle has sweeping lines that draw the eye, the gray castle is blocky, like an architectural representation of the dwarf man. It is as if the same eye has created both.

On the right is a castle equally as beautiful as the first, though slightly smaller. Between the gables of this castle are floating bridges dangling crystals like Spanish moss off a southern tree.

He sees her eyes alight on the sparkles of the hanging bridges and widen. "He really does have a flair for the beautiful. I often wonder if he created you, but then I remember none of us did."

"Who has a flair for the beautiful?"

"My brother. He is the personification of art."

"And that in the middle?" She points to the most imposing of the three castles.

"That is me. A cross between the dark and the light, to be dramatic about it. Of course, I use the word dark loosely. It is not really dark, just sort of Gothic."

He laughs to himself about using the term Gothic. It was he, of course, that inspired such movements in human artists. Dreams are, after all, the source of all inspiration.

"It's my favorite." It really is her favorite. The one on the right is startling in its beauty, but it is almost too beautiful. Morrigan has become accustomed to darkness in her life. The one on the left suits those dark comforts. However, it is too dark. It is ugly in every way.

He anticipates where her thoughts are going. "That." he spits "belongs to the Fiend." he doesn't bother to call this one his brother, though Morrigan figures this is the second brother he mentioned the last time she saw him. He could feel a near uncontrollable anger well up inside him and decided to quell it . . . for now.

"Where are we?"

"At my home."

"Where is that?" She turns to face him and read his features. He pulls a face that makes it clear he is unwilling to be specific.

"The same place we always are, really. It's just the center of it. There . . . " he gestures toward the gates "is where everything you see when you come to me leaves this place."

Morrigan doesn't push it. "It is truly wonderful." She means it. The sky is half sunshine, mostly over the castle of crystals. The other half is darkness, stars and aurora. It meets over the castle of the Winged Man.

Without speaking, he takes her hand and walks them off the terrace upon which they stand. They take a lengthy white marble staircase, laced with gold to the milk white cobblestones that lead to the castles. As they walk, a huge white phoenix sweeps down from the castle of crystals and lands before them in the path. The Winged Man smiles, ruffles his wings at it and it flies back from whence it came.

Morrigan gets the idea that some message has passed between the castle and her companion. She looks nervously at the gray castle, hoping that no message will emit forth from it. She senses that nothing from there will make her more comfortable in this moment. They continue walking until he scoops her up in his arms and flies her half way up the length of the middle castle and lets go.

For a sickening second, she thinks he has dropped her to die and then she remembers where she is. When she catches him, flying herself, she delicately plucks a feather from one of his wings and tucks it in the strap of her flowing emerald gown. She just then realizes the quality of the clothing she is wearing. It is much like her previous gown, but shimmering green rather than blue. She is so caught up in staring at it that the Winged Man has caught her and dragged her onto a balcony before she looks away.

It seems an unspoken rule that she will not speak of what is happening on the "other" side. She thinks perhaps he knows, but this is happy, that is not. She does not want to ruin it. Besides, she still has no idea who this Winged Man is, if more than her imagination, or whether he concerns himself with the Eric thing. She knows nothing what he was capable of. She knows he took vengeance on the living Eric, seemingly on her behalf and she knows that the two of them have some kind of relationship, but how deeply he feels it is a mystery.

Here, in this moment, away from the threat of the Eric thing, all Morrigan wants is to spend time with this man. His mouth, now red rather than blue, looks inviting in its plump, childish, yet ageless set. She kisses him.

The shy aspect of her nature kicks in when he turns her by grasping her waist and pressing her against the railing, slightly bent with his form against her back from thigh to shoulder. She knows there is something different about this place. It isn't like being intimate outside where she lives, but still, she feels exposed and he senses it, lifting her effortlessly once again and walking her into a room draped with shining green fabric, much like that which she is wearing. Everywhere, like their rocky hideaway, there are large cushions that invite one to relax upon them.

He doesn't set her down as they enter the room, but rather walks toward a particularly cushion-ridden area and asks her, quite seriously, if she is okay with this. She knows he is asking how comfortable she is after the events of the past week, but here, she can't feel the soreness that still lingers.

"I should have waited for exactly this, but yes, I am comfortable."

The dreaminess that is inherent in her nightmares has fled, for she is not in her nightmares. The corners of the room are completely in focus. The lines of his face and body are clearer than ever. She knows what she wants, not the tenderness of their last encounter or the detachment of his encounter with that other woman, nor the horrible experience she had with Eric. She wants something carnal, something utterly significant.

She bites his shoulder, half gently, half hungrily. She grips his tucked back wings, then runs her tongue up his shoulder and neck so her mouth is just below his ear. She feels him tense completely, waiting a moment to savor this in case it goes terribly wrong and whispered, "I love you."

The result is explosive. His strong arms hold her up while he manages to touch her face and kiss her mouth and eyes. He lays her on the bed without removing his hands from her body, leans his upper torso back from hers slightly, looks her full in the face, grips the chest of her dress and rips it all the way down to her navel. He nibbles, bites and licks every inch of exposed skin he reveals as he moves her dress out of the way.

Morrigan sees her feather slip out of her strap and fall to the pillow. She tucks it in her hair, afraid she will lose it.

He kisses her stomach hard, pressing his face into the flat softness he finds there. He scoops her buttocks beneath with his hands and pushes her waist even harder against his face. "Love you too, Morri." he whispers.

Her hands tangle in his hair. The pleasure/pain of being so close to him and so open and free is overwhelming. She tugs and he gets the idea, moving back up her body and flipping himself so he is beneath her. He doesn't relinquish his hold on her, though. All she can do is tuck her knees against his sides and press her thighs into his waist. She can feel his too large hardness pressing against her through the fabric at her waist. He raises his hips so they can rub together with more pressure. She reaches down with one hand and pushed the fabric out of the way. As he thrusts again, he is surprised to feel her warm moisture against his bare cock. His eyes fly open and he groans.

Morrigan slides herself up and down the length of him without allowing entrance. Her hips rock back and forth and she touches him all over his powerful chest and shoulders. Finally, she lifts her knees, so her feet find their way beside him and stands. He stares up at her, taking in her beautiful face looking down at him and the expanse of creamy skin that leads all the way down to her stomach. She pulls the straps of her dress down her arms and lets the material pool at her waist. He sits up and pulls it the rest of the way down, lifting her by the legs with one arm to pull the fabric completely off of her.

He can hear Morrigan's sharp intake of breath as he puts his lips between her legs and kisses her there for a moment before standing up with her in his arms and lowering her so her legs are wrapped around his waist. She gives him a smug smile that says, "Anytime now." He groans and lowers her back onto the bed. She is on her back now and he is pressed against her, waiting for something. She says, "Now, please." and he slides himself into her with some difficulty. He moves very slowly, acutely aware that they do not exactly fit properly. She doesn't notice. She is ready and this is a dream. Nothing can hurt her here, not even him.

He has a hard time holding back, so she lifts her hips, pressing him fully into her and lets out a moan of pleasure. This is all either of them need. They move passionately against each other until he lets go inside of her with a tremendous moan. He kisses her and put his hand on her face as she watches the very slight blue of his skin completely disappear. They both smile as they kissed and don't move for quite a long time -- perhaps hours, though Morrigan could never keep track of the passage of time here.

~ ~ ~ ~ ~ ~ ~ ~ ~ ~

She woke up on Monty's couch. She was instantly a mixture of happy and sad. Tears ran down her face for a moment before she got up to take a bath. She grabbed a towel from her suitcase, her bag of hygiene products and some clothes to change into and headed for the bathroom.

The bath was hot and relaxed her still tense muscles. She saw that the bruising was starting to fade and was happy that she would no longer have to be reminded of the incident every time she undressed. However, it also reminded her of the issue hanging over her head. She decided to push the thought aside and try to sort everything out tomorrow. She would go to the Doc for her appointment. Then, she would go to the lawyer and have the papers drawn up for the exchange with Monty.

She was thinking about the situation with Monty and the situation with her life when she heard Monty come in the front door.

"Morrigan?"

"In here." she said without thinking. The two of them changed in the locker room enough times that nudity was not an issue for them in the slightest.

He opened the door with a bottle of Jack in his hands and two cups. "You up for it?" he asked, placing the bottle and glasses on the vanity without looking at her.

"Most definitely."

He poured both of them a glass of the whiskey and turned to hand her one. "Jesus Christ, Morrigan. What the fuck happened to you?"

She looked down, realizing that it would look worse to him than it would to her. "I had a skiing accident when I was in Finland."

"Wow. Do you need anything?"

"No, really. It is healing. I didn't break anything."

"Lucky fuck."

"Yeah, I know."

They sat there drinking in silence for a moment, then Morrigan decided to get out of the tub. "Get out, Monty. I have to get dressed."

He ruffled her hair with one hand and walked out. She dried and dressed quickly, noticing as she dried herself between her legs that she was sore there. What the hell?

As she stepped out of the bathroom into the hallway, she heard a commotion in the living room. She grabbed the bottle of Jack off the vanity and ran down the hall to the living room. There, she saw him.

The Eric thing was standing in the middle of the living room advancing toward

Monty, who stood opposite the Eric thing and the now shattered living room window. What the fuck was with this thing? Monty's knife set was on the coffee table, probably there to be brought for sharpening the next day. Monty lunged for the knives at the same time Eric lunged for him.

Eric grabbed Monty by the neck from behind and flung him across the room, the knife set still rolled carefully in it's black case on the table. Morrigan made for the table and Eric, who had turned his attention to her. She leapt onto the table and kicked the knives in Monty's direction, at the same time swinging the bottle at the Eric things head. It didn't break as she had imagined it would. It made a loud thunk, but did nothing to stop the monster's progress.

He swiped at Morrigan with one supernaturally strong arm. It caught her on the shoulder and knocked her back onto the couch. Jumping on top of her, he made for her throat. She felt the constriction in her windpipe and kicked and punched as hard as she could. As the light started to turn to darkness, she heard a gurgling sound and felt the hands around her neck relax. Light came back into her vision and she noticed a French knife sticking out of the front of Eric's neck and a viscous pus-colored liquid dripping from the wound. The knife must have penetrated all the way from the back and severed whatever was holding the creature's head up because it rolled to the side. Morrigan could see that the light had not left the monster's eyes. She rolled out from under him with some effort, snatched her keys off the table and put her arm around Monty, pulling him off the Eric thing. The gurgling continued and its legs started to move. She saw that Monty's leg was noticeably broken and so supported him as they struggled out the door. She didn't bother closing it, knowing it would solve nothing.

"Morrigan. I need to go to the hospital."

"I know, Monty." she said as they continued down the hall to the elevator. "Do you have your cell phone?"

He reached in to his pocket and withdrew his cell phone, smiling at her through his pain. "Yep."

She got him in the elevator, sat him down and hit the close door button. She could feel Eric following them and wanted a head start. "Call 911." He was already doing it.

In a moment of self preservation, Morrigan hit the alarm in the elevator as the doors opened on the first level. It would draw people out and put them in danger, but her main concern was Monty. If she was honest with herself, she loved the carefree, competent cook. She wasn't going to let him die because of her.

She pulled Monty out into the lobby by scooping him under the armpits as he spoke to the woman on the other end of the telephone. "Yes, the intruder is still in my apartment." Morrigan doubted that. "I think I killed him." Morrigan doubted that too. "We called about the same guy yesterday." He gave the woman his address and then told her he would be at the hospital. She apparently asked him to wait there, an ambulance would be there soon. He refused and hung up. "Get me out of here, Morrigan. I'm going to be sick."

"I'm working on it, buddy."

The Winged Man

Chapter 13

Bliss.

The Winged Man with his vast responsibilities found himself again removed from them because of a single women -- Morrigan. His mind caressed her name. His body became defined by a warm rush of feeling. His constitution was like that of others like him. He was obsessive. He was capable of falling so deeply in love as to never recover.

It had happened to one of his kind in his presence. Sadly, it had ended with the demise of his mortal beloved. So far, the broken hearted lover had spent the rest of eternity pining for her. He probably could have had her back, but he was also petty, as was he who held her in his realm. Neither would budge and so the girl was trapped away from the object of her affection and away from the mortal world she had so loved.

The Winged Man was much more lucky. Morrigan hated the mortal world in which she lived. She didn't know her feelings as hate quite yet, but she would. The Winged Man was ready to murder his dark brother for his childish tormenting of Morrigan. He knew that the Fiend meant to kill her. However, it did serve one purpose. It brought Morrigan closer to choosing his world over hers. He set these thoughts aside and concentrated on his happiness. It had taken so long for it to come to this.

Instead of delivering his creations with some diversity, as he normally would, people around the world dreamed of love. He knew his brother was handling the nightmares, though he shouldn't be. The Fiend was very angry. Surely, someone would notice eventually, probably the Artist, but the Winged Man did not care. Here, a woman dreamed she lay with a beautiful, kind, tender, unknown man in a cabin sanctuary in a corrupt world while the Fiend tried to penetrate the dream with his dreary creations. There, a boy dreamed of being at the park with his loving mother. The Fiend could not corrupt such a dream. Every dream was beautiful to the Winged Man, but reminded him of Morrigan's current absence. He wished she would fall to sleep as he continued his machinations.

He doled out comfort and shared all the sweetness he felt with the sleeping world. He wanted to rush out of his world and into hers, but he had business to handle here first and creating these dreams helped him focus. He sat in the cushioned room, painting rainbows, flowers, love, perfection with his mind and sending him out into the snow globes of dreams and nightmares that made up the infinite possibilities of his realm. His eyes were closed and his wings stretched out behind him as he breathed slowly in an out, reaching out to the minds of mortals and giving them every tenderness they desired. There were those who desired that which he would never allow in his state of mind and he left those sleepers dreamless. Let them enjoy their depravity during their waking hours when he did not have to be privy to their thoughts.

"Music" he thought suddenly. That was what he was missing. The room filled with an instrumental score he remembered hearing in someone's mind and finding beautiful. There were no instruments to create the music anywhere near him. He was able to project all of his wishes outside of himself here. Oftentimes, he tormented himself, but tonight, he had realized that his lot need not torment him forever. He realized that he could share his eternity with someone other than just his brothers, who really just reflected the inequities of his existence back at him. How trapped he was in eternity.

The music drew the Artist, who entered the room in his true form. When he entered the dreams of others, he was unrecognizable for the stunning creature that he was. The Winged Man adored his brother and knew he could never stay sane without him.

"Brother, do you mind if I join you?"

"Please do." the Winged Man was able to interact with the Artist without pausing in his work.

The Artist draped his lean figure over a nearby cushion and began helping the Winged Man build perfect dreams. His knack for delicate beauty really lent an extra element to the dreams and the Winged Man became even more content. The Artist's skill was second only to his elder brother the Winged Man. He was less troubled than the Winged Man, though and perhaps more suited to the work, but it fell to the Winged Man in its entirety when he was here. The Fiend disobeyed on occasion, such as today. His dark personality did not give well to the talents of his brothers. The Winged Man was more skilled at both nightmares and dreams than his brothers, but the Fiend hated being bored. In fact, he hated nearly everything.

~~~~~~~~~~

More than fifteen years ago, the Fiend had been wandering through his nightmares outside of the castle complex. The Winged Man was taking a break in the mortal world. He often did so to get a grip on human nature, so he would be better at his work. The Fiend saw a young girl flitting between the circles of nightmares that floated everywhere around him. He was baffled. Where was her nightmare or dream? Why was she entering those of others and essentially wandering around in their realm? How was she doing it?

At first, the Fiend was intrigued by the small child. He entered the nightmares himself and tailed her. Then, he saw that nothing in the nightmares bothered her. He saw that she was content, playing with deformed trees, gazing disinterestedly upon the tortured bodies of zombies in the nightmare of a twelve-year-old boy who had watched a horror film while his parents argued in the next room. It was then that he became angry. He tried to scare her, but he couldn't penetrate her mind. He did not know what frightened her.

For months, he would seek her out and bombard her with all of the horrors he could pick from the minds of other girls her age. None of it worked. In fact, it almost seemed as if she could command the things he was sending her way. It was subtle and he imagined he was going crazy often. It was impossible. How could she control what he created? His anger increased. When the Winged Man returned, the Fiend continued his forays into the nightmares that the Winged Man created. She could control those even less. It was so subtle as to be undetectable. The fear never came, though. She wasn't afraid of either of their creations.

Eventually, the Winged Man noticed that the Fiend was invading his nightmares without consulting him or working with him. He entered the gray castle one night and demanded to know what was going on.

"What are you doing, Fiend?"

He was not angry, at first, just curious.

Always covetous of his secrets, the Fiend shooed him away.

This took the Winged Man aback. "You dare? Tell me what is going on now!" The command in his voice was palpable and the Fiend knew it was best not to ignore it, but his propensity for secrets and his curiosity about this girl won out.

"No, brother. Are we not allowed any freedom here?"

This angered the Winged Man. "You are not here to be free! None of us are. We are bound by our responsibilities. Do not shirk yours."

The Fiend scoffed, "I have no responsibilities right now. I am merely spending time out there." He gestured through the window at the gates outside. He then scuttled like a spider away from his brother and hid in the corner. "Besides" he hissed, "You will interfere."

The Winged Man knew something was happening and it was up to him to control it. His brother's isolation and refusal to conform to his fate angered him vastly. "Tell me now, Fiend!" He roared. "This is your last chance."

"No," he said with some satisfaction.

That day, the Winged Man destroyed the gray castle in his anger. He then bound the Fiend to the gates. "You will stay there until I figure out why you are doing this. Even then, I may decide to keep you there."

Always convinced that his brother was an imbecile, despite all of the evidence to the contrary, the Fiend retorted, "I'll be stuck here forever then, you daft tyrant."

"Tyrant?! Why I have to deal with you at all will forever be a mystery to me. Stay there and rot for all I care." the Winged Man did feel a twinge of guilt, seeing his helpless deformed brother like this, but there was nothing he could do. He could not let him run rampant, forever flitting from nightmare to nightmare. People would notice him. Eventually, he would create some ridiculous myth on Earth.

The Artist was sympathetic with both of his brothers, of course, though he stayed out of it, other than to look at both of them meaningfully whenever he passed.

Knowing that his brother the Fiend would only enter the nightmares, he started his search for something amiss among the dreams. He paid close attention to every detail in every dream he created. He watched the people in them, those he created and those who were dreaming in them. He watched their reactions and found nothing. Nothing was there.

He then began his search of the nightmares and it wasn't long before he started to see a familiar figure in all of them. A small girl, with big beautiful eyes and flowing black hair. He had seen her before, but now she intrigued him. Why would she stay here in the world of nightmares? Why couldn't he read her and make her a beautiful dream filled with ponies? Why couldn't he even build her a nightmare of her own. It was as if she could travel to this place in its entirety without being confined to her own globes of unconsciousness. After time, he began building her nightmares anyway. She never entered the dreams that he built for her. Several years passed and he had built her a vast complex of nightmares. He couldn't confine her to them, but he saw that she preferred to be in the nightmares that were not inhabited by others. She didn't like stumbling on remnants of the real world in her sleeping state.

She grew into a young woman as he created entire worlds for her, some that she has yet to see and some that she frequents. It was only a few months before he started joining her in her dreams. She seemed to enjoy his company and he began to love her over time. By the time she was a young woman, he had figured out that she was actually as much a part of his realm as hers, if not more so. There had to be some way to get her here and keep her here, but he would have to make a deal with another of his kind whom he would rather not make deals with.

He released the Fiend the moment he knew what was going on and demanded that he stay away from the girl. Over the years, the Fiend had kept his promise only part of the time. Because he was relatively harmless to the girl, the Winged Man did not bother him about his indiscretions. When he followed her into a dream while the Winged Man was away, he would try to terrify her to no avail. Things like the angry dwarf and the bound diners were his specialty. The Winged Man laughed at his efforts more often than not. He watched as the Fiend became infuriated with the girl. Then, she became a woman and the Fiend's eyes had changed. The Winged Man saw a perverted version of what he felt for her in those eyes.

"Stay away from her or I will bind you to those gates for all of eternity."

"I don't know what you are going on about. Honestly, I think you are spending too much time with her. It's making you insane. Just let it go. She is mortal. She will die soon and things will go back to normal."

The Winged Man looked around him at the castle the Fiend had painstakingly rebuilt. "I will tear it all down again and again if you continue with your obsession."

The Fiend laughed long and hard. "My obsession. You're deluded. It is you who are obsessed."

"Perhaps, but I am not also deranged."

He feigned hurt. "Deranged? How cruel of you to say that."

"I mean it, Fiend. She will be here with me, whether you like it or not."
"I'll not say another word to you about it, brother."

In a moment of innocence, the Winged Man had heard the sincerity in his voice and thought it was all encompassing. It was not. The Fiend had other plans. Plans that would come to fruition on the day of Eric's murder.

Chapter 14

The Winged Man was sitting in his castle, waiting for a glimpse of Morrigan. He spent most of his time like this, idly doing his work and waiting for her to appear. Things were moving forward for the two of them. He was happy, content believing that his plans will go precisely as he hoped. He daydreamed of her, because of course he did not sleep and therefore, could not dream. He could however, create dreams with a facsimile of her in them. He contemplated doing so now, but just then his brother's phoenix entered the room.

"Don't go anywhere. I am on my way." it thought at him in the voice of the Artist. The Winged Man wondered what this was about, but did exactly what his brother had asked, despite that he had become fond of the idea of leaving to spend time with a dream version of Morrigan while he awaited the real thing.

In what would have been a few minutes, had The Winged Man kept track of time, the Artist entered his room. "We have to talk."

"Sit, brother." he gestured to a large, Gothic throne-like chair across from his own.

"As much as I would like to, now is not the time. It may be best if you stand."

Now the Winged Man was worried.

"Speak." He commanded. He rarely ordered this brother around, but could tell by the wary sadness in his voice that he had something to tell him, something that he would not like.

"I don't know how to say it. I have a message from the Emissary. It is better if you see for yourself."

A feeling of dread was passing over the Winged Man. He got the sense that this had everything to do with the woman with whom he had fallen in love. His brothers knew of his obsession and by extension, so did every other being like them. If the Emissary had a message for him, it had to come from up there. He was either being reprimanded or something had happened. He doubted the former and began to believe the latter was the case.

"It's her, isn't it?" The Winged Man asked and the Artist paused. "Tell me, dammit! At least that much, please."

"Yes, it is. Her mortality remains an issue, but she is still alive. Do not look so damn tortured. You have to hold it together."

While they spoke, they went to the castle of the Artist, skipping the stairs and flying up to a bridge leading to a vast tower with the Artist liked to spend time with his brothers, though he received very little of their time, on average. There, in a pool of water, was his method of communication with the Emissary. The fleet footed man would stop by, drop a stone in the liquid and leave. The stone would turn to mist, which would in turn swirl into messages that often consisted of visions of moments passed that others wanted the Artist to see. Otherwise, it would simply emit the voice of another with a message for the Artist.

The Winged Man rushed into the room. The Artist, out of respect for his brother's sanity, rushed ahead of him and grabbed a silver staff off the wall. With the staff, he stirred the clear pool of water until a mist began to appear in tendrils. Just a few moments later, it showed the start of Eric's encounter with Morrigan in the igloo.

"Why would you show me this?" the Winged Man shuddered as he watched Morrigan and the man have sex.

"Because something changed. Keep watching."

"Changed?" He was instantly concerned again. Not for himself, but for Morrigan.

The Artist did not respond, he just looked meaningfully and mournfully at the glassy surface of this echo of events past. The Winged Man watched along with him and, as the image changed, he changed. He roared and his innocent visage became that of a demon. His wings became bat-like and his fingers emitted claws. His head shook back and forth furiously, but his eyes never left the message before him. He watched, chest heaving, until the man left Morrigan alone.

"How long ago?" He hissed at the Artist.

The Artist, completely un-bothered by this monstrous transition, replied, "Moments in her world."

The muscles on the demon's chest tensed as it dug its claws into the ground and turned back toward the door. It turned its head briefly and almost apologetically said, "You will handle things in my absence and keep him in check. I will not be long at all."

The Artist nodded.

The Fiend listened to all of this from outside the door and dropped off the bridge just as the demon came out. When the Winged Man left, he skittered up the side of the tower and walked in to see the Artist sitting cross-legged in the corner, clearly doing his other brother's bidding.

"Hello," the Fiend uttered as he walked in. "Something has happened with the girl?"

"Yes" the Artist offered, without opening his eyes. "See for yourself." he saw no harm in filling the Fiend in on the situation with Eric and Morrigan. He would find out some way or another and the Artist hardly saw how this could be fodder for the Fiend, but the Artist rarely saw what his more sinister brother was capable of.

The Fiend watched the message, enjoying it much more than the Winged Man would have allowed. The Fiend had feelings for Morrigan, just like the Winged Man. However, his feelings of love were always mixed with a sadistic need, as evidenced by his constant attempts to sabotage his brothers. He watched as Eric beat Morrigan and his eyes gleamed. She had never been so lovely to him. However, he noticed something that the Winged Man had missed, her eyes were glazed over. She did not feel it. "Who did that?"

The Artist knew what he had spoke of, but had not bothered to mention it to the Winged Man. He would see again, over and over again, and notice the next time he obsessed over it.

"Someone was watching over her. The Winged Man is not the only person who knows she is special, as you know personally, I'm afraid."

The Fiend huffed and turned back to the water. The images were gone. It was over. He reached for the staff. The Artist heard the noise and suspected what his brother wanted -- to see her pain again. "Put that down and leave my house."

Another huff and the Fiend skittered out of the room on all fours. He did not return to his castle. He was on his way to a realm just outside of his. While the Winged Man did his work, the Fiend would do some of his own.

~~~~~~~~~~

The Winged Man found Eric walking in the snow. His truck had not started, another trick that the Winged Man missed, but that had come from a friend. Because of this, Eric was walking toward the more populated area of the resort. It took every ounce of the Winged Man's strength to keep the demon trapped in his human shell when he saw Eric. Even still, he felt some of its raw power emanating from him. Good, he would need that.

"It's late to be wandering around." he said in a smooth, seductive voice.

Always the man's man, Eric smiled. "Look who's talking, buddy."

That rankled, but he chuckled to himself. Buddy, indeed. "I'm going ice swimming."

"Really?! Ballsy. I like it."

"Would you like to tag along? The hole is right there." He gestured just a few feet away to a rectangle of metal railing.

The Winged Man could tell by looking at Eric's face that he was pondering the idea of leaving his truck in front of Morrigan's igloo while he hung around the hotel and found it was a bad idea. This pissed the Winged Man off and the events Morrigan saw later played out. It took him only a minute to dispatch this disgusting piece of human shit. Then, he became sad and the demon fled, him with it. He returned to his realm shattered. The moment he alit within the gates, the phoenix landed in front of him. "She's here." He nodded his thanks at the bird and toward his brother's castle. Then, he left to find Morrigan.

He arrived in her nightmare, one that he had created years ago and that she seemed to enjoy, only moments after she did. He called to her, unable to help himself. Even here, away from the pain she had just endured, she looked blank, like something had been stolen from her. Something had. The thought propelled him. He scooped her up and sat with her while he wept silently and she drifted in thoughts unknown.

Chapter 15

He wandered through a dense blackness at the edge of the dream realm. Every so often a scratching or a slithering brushed his skin. He embraced the sensation. "This is where I belong," he thought. "This is what I am working for." He tried to remind himself that patience would be his only hope as the excitement rose inside of him. He must first make allies of his enemies.

The darkness ended where the faint green glow of a river penetrated the viscous lack of color. He scurried to the water's edge and looked in at the macabre scene there -- souls trapped, pressing against each other, fighting against the water's movement and each other in a hopeless struggle against their fate. He laughed out loud. The sound was dry and scratching, much more like the sound escaping a newly dead corpse than actual laughter. He enjoyed the view for a moment before hustling along the water's edge toward a black mountain in the distance. His destination was in the heart of that mountain.

He was allowed in to see the man who could do what he needed. He sat in a cavernous room upon a throne of body parts. Next to him sat a delicately beautiful woman who looked detached from her surroundings. The faint glow she gave off showed that she did not belong there, but her hand was caught in the claw like hand of the man the Fiend had come to see.

"Fiend, I wasn't expecting to see you here." He leaned forward, revealing a long face with sunken black eyes and wide red mouth filled with needle like teeth. "What brings you here, my shifty friend?"

The Fiend ignored the insult and the suspicion in the dark man's voice. "I need a favor."

"You need a favor? Favors aren't my favorite." He smiled a frightening smile, devoid of any real emotion.

"I am aware of that. I am willing to make a trade."

"Then it is not really a favor, making me more likely to cooperate. What is it that you want, Fiend?"

"First, I would like a man to come back as . . . something else."

"First?" the dark man sighed. "Why?'

"Because he would go after someone whom I want to see terrorized."

"Why?"

This was frustrating; the Fiend took a deep breath, "Because I have never been able to succeed at doing this with nightmares."

"Really?" This time the dark man smiled with true pleasure. He enjoyed seeing the insectile Fiend put out.

"Really." the Fiend replied begrudgingly.

"Find him on your way out. If you can find him before your brother discovers what you are doing, you get what you want. Remember, this is not like putting your nightmarish creations out there, Fiend. His actions will have real repercussions." It was worded like a warning, but the dark man sounded glad of the potential harm caused by his deal with the Fiend.

"I understand."

"You will need this." he handed the Fiend a jagged shard of what looked like dirty quartz. The Fiend greedily tucked it within his robes. "You said first before. Tell me the second and do not expect me to be so generous this time."

"I want you to entrap a soul here that would not be destined for this realm after death."

"Not destined for this realm? *All* are destined for this realm."

"Not this one."

The dark man leaned back in his throne. "Tell me everything. Proceed knowing that I am fully aware we are talking about the same person as before, my lecherous friend."

The Fiend explained how Morrigan could manipulate nightmares and how he believed she was more than mere mortal, that she was to be part of the dream realm. He left it at that.

"There is something you are leaving out. If you want me to direct this woman here, you'll have to tell all. I have no idea how she came to be the way she is. This could anger some of us, which may not be to my benefit. This is sounding more and more like a favor."

The Fiend came out with it, "My brother loves her -- the Winged Man, that is."

He left out his own feelings for her. That would reveal too much.

"Well, that is interesting. Your brother is quite different from us. Treading the waters between dark and light. He represses you a lot doesn't he?"

The dark man's eagerness to take part in this rebellion was becoming clear. He enjoyed the Fiend's torment and would enjoy even more to see both brother's tormented. He had nothing to gain save a sick pleasure, but it did break up the tedium of this place. "What do I get in trade?" he inquired.

"You get sole possession of the one thing the Winged Man loves in this world. I would find pleasure in that simple fact myself . . ." much more pleasure than he would let on to this dark man ". . . but you get an added bonus. A bargaining chip, if you will. You can keep her forever and always have that power over the Winged Man."

"And if he becomes no longer enamored of her?"

"That will not happen." he nodded toward the woman seated next to the dark man. "You know that as well as I."

The dark man glanced toward what he saw as his only weakness. He both loved and hated her, but only revealed possessiveness to others. He was almost surprised that the Fiend picked up on his sick devotion to the woman. He didn't let it show.

"See to it that she dies." With that simple sentence, he was done. The Fiend had his compliance. He was being dismissed. Without bothering to say thank you he left. Such niceties between the two were pointless. Neither meant it or excepted it. Each was scheming their own schemes and each knew it.

Surprisingly, it did not take the Fiend long to find Eric among the murdered. His brother was surely still otherwise occupied, off somewhere with Morrigan. The idea that they were together rankled. Each thought of him made the Fiend's disposition blacker.

He thrust the jagged rock down Eric's throat, as the other gurgled, still stuck in the pain of his last moments. He then pulled a special coin out of his robes, handed it to Eric and directed him toward the river. The monstrous reanimated murder victim wandered off in that direction with a new awareness in its eyes.

Had the Fiend thought about it, he would have realized that the dark man had wanted him to find Eric, had indeed known precisely who Eric was and much more of what was going on than he had let on. However, the Fiend had not thought about it, had disregarded the relationships his kind kept with one another and the news that traveled fast among them, as he himself had very little wish to communicate with anyone. He preferred his existence to be uninterrupted by the company of others, unless they were there to entertain him with their pain or to do his bidding, as he had thought the dark man had been tricked into doing.

Chapter 16

Days pass.

The Winged Man spends them all distraught, angry, emotional, leaving his true work to his brothers and waiting for Morrigan to sleep. He hides from everything in an attempt to relieve himself of all of his pain without revealing his weakness to the Fiend. He has no idea just how much he has already revealed and how much his brother plans to utilize it. He finally sees Morrigan, who manages to lessen his pain, but only by a fraction. His guilt remains, only slightly stronger than his fear that she will never come to love him. How could she? She still isn't sure if he is real. It might even be better that way, given that knowing he is real would reveal just how much he had let her down.

He should have always been watching, always assuring that she was safe in the world he let her stay in. He thought it was for her sake, but what was he really doing? What was he waiting for? The truth is that he was waiting for her full acceptance. He was waiting for her to come into herself, as it were. See herself for who she was. Rid herself of the anxiety that tormented her. The constant imagined threat of insanity looming over her head.

He knew that her fears were unfounded, but he didn't want to thrust reality on her too soon, afraid that she would be unhappy in the new life he hoped to give her. He assumed that if she died too soon, he could remedy that, but what made him so sure? With every passing minute, her anxiety became his. His fears became more real. Her ignorance of the things she should truly fear became more fodder for his guilt. It was agony and he continued to live in it. Because of this, he planned to attempt immersing her more into the life they should have together when he saw her again. He planned to show her the better side of what could be. He still could not show her that it was possible to live on without ever going back to her life. Not yet, but he could test her a little more. See if it wasn't he who was delusional after all.

After his meeting with Morrigan, he sulked back to the inner sanctum of his realm. He began his work again, but only with the help of his sweet brother. He gave no more work to the Fiend upon his return, meaning to handle the nightmares himself, in case he caught a glimpse of Morrigan. The last thing he wanted was for the Fiend to see her first. He was tired of the Fiend's tricks, but unaware just how far they went.

He stood inside of the gates, pondering their significance, wondering what it would be like without them and taking a brief break when the Artist summoned him. The Artist sat in a field of his own flowers, white with golden veins lacing

the petals. There was no grass amidst them, but rather a soft aquamarine-colored substance with a finish not unlike polished rocks.
The Winged Man sat comfortably next to him and thanked him for his help.

"You're welcome, brother. I am bored without any work to do. Without your obsession . . . " he cleared his throat, though that was rather unnecessary for a being such as him ". . . I would still be bored."

"I will remember not to hog everything in the future."

"It is in your nature to be a perfectionist and do these things yourself. That is not to mention the fact that they are your responsibility. That we are able to help you when we can is fortunate, but it is not the Fiend and I who were made for this. That is unimportant, however, and not the reason I called for you."

"I assumed as much."

"We have another problem. This time, I believe it involves our wayward brother."

"Go on."

"You see, I have been told that a recently dead man has come back to life. You, of course, remember the last time this happened?"

The Winged Man did remember. He wished he did not. An entire army disappeared on their march home from a hard won battle. No one knew what had happened to them. They could not have known that the army they had defeated had made a deal with a very bad being to come back to life. The mortal army was slaughtered in the wilderness, their bodies so destroyed as to be nearly undetectable. Thus far, there had been no nearly about it. Now the two armies spent all of eternity hashing out their old problems. None of them knew it was over. The deal struck by the initially defeated army had only served as entertainment for a bored god.

"I do, Artist. I assume this has something to do with us? I know that your sympathies run deep, but I cannot interfere on the behalf of mortals." he paused "Except on rare occasions. Forgive me, I know I am selfish, but I would risk too much to anger he who must be responsible for this."

"That is the problem, brother. This is a rare occasion and a mighty similar one."

The Winged Man immediately stood. "What is it now?" he gripped his head in both hands, imagining correctly what was coming.

"The man you killed has come back. As with all such occurrences, he is fixated on his last grievance, so to speak. We know he cannot send the undead after you, so he has done the next best thing. However, if you took a moment, as I have, you would realize that it is not he who is the originator of this problem."

The Winged Man did not let forth his anger. He had had enough of that for now. Instead, a quiet energy poured out of him, shattering the pretty flowers in the field. His shoulders slumped as it happened.

"It's all right. I will fix them. You will have, by now, realized that she is currently in no immediate danger or I would not be sitting here with you. He did find her, but she escaped and has left the vicinity. So far, he does not know where she has gone, only who she has gone with."

"Who she has gone with? Who would she trust?"

"That chef you practically haunted the first week he worked for her."

"It was . . ." he spat out "Oh, forget it. I left him alone after that and it seems he is safe for her. What now?"

"We have to talk to the Fiend. I think this is his doing and I am sure you do by now too. You have seen him slinking around here, eying you with more hatred than is usual for him. You must know why he is mad at you and what he seeks."

"I do."

"So, we either dispatch this thing and potentially expose you to the anger of another or we have the Fiend put a stop to it and save us all the trouble."

"A sound plan. I would rather do it myself."

"I know."

"You are right in your thinking, of course. Shall I?"

"Perhaps I should."

"Soon, please?"

"Now works for me."

With that, the Artist disappeared from view. Out of respect for his brother and anger at himself for being so irritable and quick to react lately, he spent the time his brother was gone carefully fixing the field he had destroyed. He was sure he came close to his brother's perfect flowers, but such delicate things were always best left in the Artist's hands. He sighed. At least the Artist would have less to do when he strolled back in here, which could be centuries from now, given the sheer vastness of their sanctuary.

By the time the Artist and the Winged Man met to discuss the Fiend's involvement in the fiasco, the Winged Man was in the dungeons of his castle, contemplating entrapping the Fiend there for the foreseeable future. That might get him some discouraging visits, but it would keep him out of the way until Morrigan was safe with him. The question was whether he could manage the backlash and Morrigan. He simply did not want anything else to take his attention away from her again.

The Winged Man had already seen the consequences of not diligently watching, though he also got the sense that his fickle cousins were purposely keeping their information on the mortal realm to themselves and only delivering to the Artist because jealousy regarding love was rampant among their kind, the Artist and himself excluded. It didn't matter if they were in love themselves, they couldn't stand it when others were. Spiteful to the core was most of his kind -- the Fiend second only to one.

"That would not do, brother. For self-preservation's sake, I would have to stop you -- or try." the Artist walked into the dungeon, his voice echoing from the ancient arched entryway. It was the most nightmarish area of his castle and somehow, the Artist made it less so.

"The verdict?"

"He is denying any involvement and he is lying. I had assumed he would, but sought to test his honesty on this topic first myself." he could always spot impurities, even in the Winged Man and Morrigan. He said nothing, but knew the depth of the Winged Man's feelings were a huge weakness for him, as if the chasm where his emotions welled up had the potential to be empty and dark. Given the opportunity, he could be the worst of us all, the Artist had thought when he finally put his finger on what about the Winged Man made him part frightening. Conversely, the feelings themselves were what made him part wonderful. His feelings were clear. He was honest and true to his emotions without exception.

"Well, if you are sure he is lying, I am sure he is lying and something must be done."

"Make him turn the creature off its path. Make him renege on the deal he must have made."

"That puts him in terrible danger."

The Artist sighed. "I know, but it is not more than he deserves. I do not want this for him, but he brought it on himself. Allowing whatever he is doing to play out is out of the question."

The Winged Man's mouth set in a severe line. "Obviously."

"Yes, obviously."

The Winged Man walked out on the Artist without another word. It was not rude. Extraneous words were pointless. They had spent millennia in each other's company. Pleasantries had fled not long after they had spent the length of a mortal's life together.

The Winged Man stepped out into the half day/half night that hovered over his land. He looked to the gates and concentrated for a moment. The black shadow of his demon figure, a part of him that he had cast out for the time being, floated toward him. "Make him come to me." he commanded.

It vanished and moments later could be seen floating back through the gates. A high-pitched voice made the Winged Man turn to his brother.

"Really, I much prefer that side of you. So much less contemptible. Pure and impulsive."

"As you see yourself?"

"Now, now, that question is intended as an insult, I can see. You forced me to come to you, so I assume you have something to say, similar to what the Artist has already said. Out with it so I can go in." the Winged Man knew the Fiend was uncomfortable out here, in the half-light with all of the color and splendor surrounding him. It was why he had called to him. The Winged Man was cruel in his own way. Though he would never know it, his very righteousness had helped carve his younger brother's personality.

"You know what I want to say. Fix the problem you have caused."
The Fiend bravely skittered up to his brother and stood erect in a flash of black.

"I see no problem."

The Fiend thought it was power that made others flinch when he pressed his will with merely his voice and presence. In reality, it was revulsion. He really was insectile. His eyes small and lined with red from hundreds of years hiding in darkness. Cruelty radiated from him and he was truly frightening. Only some of his kind didn't suffer this revulsion and only one human. That is part of why he had wanted the girl so badly. A test. An eternity of torment. A transformation. She would be his.

The Winged Man was one of the few who was unaffected by his brother. His own dark side left him immune from such superficial fears. The Fiend posed no threat to him, in his mind.

"It hardly matters what you see, Fiend. There is a problem and you know how to fix it. Remedy it and we will pretend it never happened."

The Fiend knew the dilemma in which he had placed his brother. He knew what was being asked of him. Go back on your deal so we do not have to suffer the indignity of a feud. Fix it so I do not have to face he who you have dealt with. Save face for us all and I will forgive. The Fiend almost spat as he analyzed his brother's meaning.

"Remedy what?"

He was goading his brother and would continue to do so forever if the Winged Man allowed it. He had surely done this with the far more tolerant Artist.

The Winged Man was not going to give him what he wanted. He did the one thing that would work or have some semblance of working. He said the one thing that would cause his brother to pause and rethink his strategy. The Winged Man did not look so far ahead as to see how his brother would work it out. He assumed his will would be done. "Do it or I will go to him myself."

The Fiend's pride could not allow that. He could not have his brother embarrass him. He did the only thing he could do, he lied. "Fine." he behaved angrily, so his brother would not suspect. It was very much lucky the Artist had left this to the two of them now or his lie would have been caught immediately. "I just wanted to have a little fun. She is so . . . immune." His face contorted with disgust for Morrigan's strength.

"It's not fun, Fiend. This is different and you know it."

He knew it all too well.

He pitched a fit to make it appear as if he would really follow his brother's instructions. He brooded in his castle for several hours. Let the time pass. The thing wasn't on to her location yet. He had plenty of time to let this play out and then seek asylum from his brother once the creature caught on to her. In fact, he could disguise his plan right among the actions he would have taken, had he obeyed his brother.

By the time he exited the castle, the Fiend was very confident that this was not even so much as a setback. He didn't let it show, though. He slinked along, his belly closer to the ground than usual. The Artist would be suspicious, but would have no recourse.

The Artist was waiting for him, sadness on his face. "You will reap your own punishment. Just because I think you deserve it does not mean I wish it upon you. I will see you when the seeds you have sown have grown, withered and died. Until then." With that, he was gone.

If there was a soft spot in the Fiend at all, it was for his brother the Artist. He had chalked it up to being able to hurt his brother so easily for all these years. A creature so sensitive is always loved by creatures as sadistic as the Fiend. That wasn't completely it, but he would never have the opportunity to realize it.

The Winged Man was nowhere to be seen, but a black bird landed on the Fiend's back as he skittered toward the adjacent realm of blackness. It sat there, a token of the Winged Man's undeserved love for the Fiend, until his darkness fled the realm.

~~~~~~~~~~

By the time the Artist and the Winged Man were alone in the Winged Man's castle, it had been hours since the Fiend left for the dark realm. If either of them were nervous, they said nothing. The Winged Man, optimistic that his brother would do the right thing in this situation, assumed Morrigan was safe. He would beat himself up later for what was happening to Morrigan and Monty as they sat there.

A few minutes into their concerted effort to bring the world beauty in its sleep, the Artist excused himself.

"This was very enjoyable. I hate to cut it short, but I have a message. I'll try to come back in a little while."

Something told the Artist this was about him -- about Morrigan.

"Do you mind if I come with you, to be sure?"

"I assumed you would. Come on."

They arrived in the room with the pool and saw a mist stirring within. Stirring the liquid showed both the Artist and his brother what was happening. Morrigan and Monty were being stalked by the Eric thing. The Winged Man's vows to hold his temper mattered not in this moment. Anger was not what he felt. He felt a tremendous feeling of guilt.

"Go now, brother. You still have time."

"I'll be leaving you alone for some time, I fear." His eyes showed that it was the least of his worries, but wanted to ensure that the Artist understood what he was undertaking.

"It will be sweet dreams for a time, won't it?" he said with a wry smile "Go. You do not have much time. It must be very angry now."

In moments, the Winged Man was standing in front of a glass lobby entrance. Inside, he saw Morrigan dragging a man across the floor. People had yet to emerge from the floors above, but the Winged Man could hear sirens in the distance. He didn't have much time.

He moved to open the door and enter the lobby. As he did, a staircase door opened to Morrigan's right and a tall, misshapen figure emerged. He was moving fast, with intent now, but so was the Winged Man. Morrigan didn't see the Eric thing. He had to distract it. Monty was staring right at him, but he figured that damage could be remedied later.

The clothing he wore tore to shreds as the demon found its home inside him once again. Unlike when he killed Eric, the entire demon emerged. He snarled loudly at the Eric thing, who stopped his advance on Morrigan and turned toward the Winged Man. The sight of the thing that had killed him took him off of Morrigan. He crouched and made to leap at the Winged Man. At this point, both Morrigan and Monty were in a hurry to leave. Monty tried to stand while Morrigan tried not to attract the attention of the two monsters before her.

What the hell was this new thing? She got the sense that it wasn't about to pounce them, so she rushed behind him to exit the lobby.

Inside, the Winged Man got one devastating blow on the Eric creature that knocked it back into the wall. He couldn't stay here to finish him off. The police were coming. He could hear the elevators working to bring witnesses down and nothing was keeping people from entering the lobby from outside at any moment.

He turned and ran for the door while the Eric thing was still incapacitated. He morphed into his human form just soon enough that he didn't destroy the doorway as he left. Morrigan was helping Monty around the corner into the parking garage.

"Stop. Let me help you!"

The Winged Man ran toward the duo. Morrigan looked terribly shocked and pleased. Monty looked simply shocked. "Morrigan, go. That guy is naked and crazy."

"He's real." was all she said.

On the run, the Winged Man picked up a struggling Monty and told Morrigan to follow him.

There was nothing he could do about Eric right now. He had to help Morrigan with her friend and get them far away for the time being. He could hunt the Eric thing later and end this nonsense once and for all.

Monty was freaking out by the time the Winged Man got him to the truck. "Morrigan, what the fuck? This guy has schizo strength, he's naked and I'm honestly not sure he isn't that fucking black monster. Run!"

"Monty, just stop kicking. We have to go."

Monty's face fell. He was becoming resigned to the fact that this situation was irredeemably FUBAR and there was nothing he could do about it. "Just stop rubbing against me, dude."

The Winged Man half-smiled, turned to place Morrigan in the truck, only to realize that she was already there. He jumped in, started it up and drove for the first time in his existence.

"I'm not going to ask you what you are doing here, if I am crazy or what is going on. However, if Monty can hold out for an extra 20 minutes, I am going to ask that you stop at the 24-hour Crestmart so I can get you some clothes."

He looked down at his nude figure and heard Monty pipe up from the back, "Yeah, you are naked, in case you haven't noticed."

The Winged Man didn't know what to say. He didn't want to freak out Morrigan's friend. This was supposed to be a big moment for him and Morrigan, so he didn't want her pal ruining that, either. Here they are, together, without her having to wonder if she is putting too much stock into her dreams. He chose to say nothing. He nodded his assent to Morrigan, who then showed him where the store was.

She went in alone, using Monty's credit card to purchase a black sweater and a pair of jeans that looked like they might be too wide and too short for the godly looking creature in her truck. They would have to suffice. Some socks and a pair of slippers that didn't look much like slippers sealed the transaction. She figured slippers would be less likely to cause an issue if they didn't fit quite right.

She handed him the sweater as she jumped into the truck. "Throw this on first. It will make you less conspicuous." Monty snorted and she ignored him. He was sweating profusely and in serious need of a doctor, but he was holding up well.

The Winged Man obeyed Morrigan immediately, slipping the sweater over his head with a somber look on his face. Here he was, being coached by her, barely saving her from Eric and endangering her even more by being suspicious in front of her friend and who knows how many others. He had seen people noticing his upper body nudity and hoped none of them had contacted the police. He assumed the police would be very busy figuring out what happened at the apartment building a few blocks away, but you never know. He didn't have time to phase in and out to get a better look at the big picture. For better or for worse, he was here, not quite mortal, but restricted in many of the same ways mortals were. He didn't wonder why Morrigan felt so anxious here.

Morrigan was looking down at the pants and looking at the Winged Man strangely.

"What?" he muttered softly.

"I might have to get out so you can stretch out and put these on. You're definitely not managing to pull on pants sitting there." It was true. His tall frame was already bent in odd shapes to fit in the large cab.

"Okay."

She handed him the pants, wondering at how she forgot to get him underwear. His height and nudity weren't the only conspicuous things about him that needed hiding. She waited outside for a moment, before he opened her door for her and tucked back into his spot.

"Monty passed out. We really need to get to a hospital."

They rushed the rest of the way, the Winged Man driving barefoot for the time being. When they got to the hospital, Morrigan went with Monty and the Winged Man said he would park the car.

She looked back at him as she was waiting for Monty to be loaded onto a gurney. "Are you staying?" She was thinking that he would leave now that the crisis was past.

"Yes, Morrigan." He was sad that she had to ask. He was sad that he was barely ever there for her. He was sad that this was the first time he was following through and he was damn sure he wasn't doing it right. He felt vulnerable and clumsy and was dreading explaining to Morrigan why he and the demon (she had not seen him enter the lobby) had arrived in such quick succession.

She rushed into the hospital with Monty, confused about the Winged Man's sad appearance, but more concerned for Monty than anything. She answered a few questions about him for intake, she was his emergency contact and had all of his information, then was forced to sit in the waiting room until news came about his condition.

Minutes later, the Winged Man entered the waiting room just right of the emergency room exit. He looked awkward, shy and not at all the confident man from her dreams, but she could tell it was him. Every feature he possessed was burned in her memory from childhood until now. She would never have mistaken him for another.

She wondered about whether she should eagerly greet him, but he looked around the waiting room at the other people there and sat in same slouched fashion as the others before she could react. He was sitting to her left. Because of his height, he had to look down and right to look at her, which he did. He said nothing and moved not at all after initially moving his head to look at her.

Morrigan fidgeted. She couldn't help it. She didn't know what to say and was afraid she would act weird if she looked at him for too long. She felt uncomfortable and imperfect here. The confidence she had with him while she was sleeping was completely lacking in this place. Her recent mishaps had sapped her of all her energy, as well. The only motivation she had left was sheer will. Will to survive, will to see Monty safe and will to move on from this.

It was 2 a.m. when the doctor came out to speak to Morrigan. She had been waiting for 45 minutes in silence by then. She didn't want to be the one to break the silence and so left it to him. He didn't oblige. He found the setting so odd and unfamiliar that he didn't want to start this way. He wanted to wait, as he always did, for the right moment.

The doctor told her that Monty had several broken ribs and a severely broken leg. The leg break was what the doctor called a "femoral shaft fracture" and would require surgery. She could go in and see Monty now, but he would be undergoing the operation shortly.

She left the Winged Man in the waiting room with a silent plea for him to stay. He stared at her and didn't move a muscle. That was as good an answer as any for her.

When she walked in, Monty was sitting up in bed, flipping listlessly through the channels on the television hanging in the corner. He looked at her by way of hello.

"Monty." she said and went over to his side. "I am so sorry about this."

"Morrigan, chill. I know it isn't your fault. Still, I don't think I can be involved anymore. Whatever is happening is beyond me. I am going to stow it away like a bad acid trip and get on with my life." He looked apologetic.

"That's fine, Monty. I was about to suggest the same thing. I'm going to go get what I have left out of my apartment and your apartment and try to relocate whatever this is to far away from here."

"I need to ask you a favor first. Actually, a few favors."

"Anything." and she meant it. One thing she and the Winged Man had in common in that moment was remorse.

"I don't want to go back to my place."
"Of course."

"Could you line me up something and get my stuff there? You can use my paycheck to get everything moved and get a place. I just don't want to go back and it looks like moving might be a heinous idea by myself."

"I can handle that. I'm going to take care of the restaurant and a few personal things when you're in surgery. I'll be back later and we can talk about a place for you."

"Thanks, Morri." his eyes were closing, so Morrigan squeezed his hand and left.

The Winged Man was waiting in the same spot she had left him. "Are you coming with me?" she asked. He stood and walked out the door with her.

~~~~~~~~~~

They had seven hours to kill before her appointment with Doc and four more before her appointment with her lawyer. After a brief, silent breakfast, they headed to Morrigan's apartment. She had spoken to the police the day before, who had said she could go back. She still wondered what she would go back to.

She parked on the curb, strangely feeling eager that it would be her last time here. She looked across at the silent figure staring at her from across the truck's bench seat.

"Listen, I don't know how much you have seen or really much of anything. I assume you understand that I am being hunted by something rather awful?" he flinched, but nodded. "Okay, whatever that is might be here. I have no idea. I have to go up and get my stuff, so I can make arrangements to leave the city. You can stay in the truck or come up, but I want you to know that coming up may be dangerous."

It felt odd talking to him like this -- like they didn't know each other, but the truth was, this Morrigan didn't know him. She had never met him before. In a way, she had only seen him in pictures or videos, to be more accurate.

He said nothing, simply opened his door and walked around to meet her on her side of the truck. He walked ahead of her as they entered the building, the

staircase, the hall and finally pushed past her when she unlocked the door to her apartment. He was hovering, she noticed, and wondered what that meant.
There was nothing in the apartment to worry about, apart from some broken glass that would be the end of her security deposit.

Morrigan grabbed as many clothes, keepsakes and toiletries as she could fit in the bags at her disposal. Nothing that was left meant anything to her, just items necessary for apartment living. All of her important paperwork was locked up in the office at Morrigan's. She was in and out in 30 minutes, without speaking or receiving a word from the Winged Man.

The next stop was Monty's apartment building. It was four o'clock in the morning by then and the place was deserted. She assumed the police would be watching the building, but knew they would have no idea to expect her. They would surely try to reach Monty, but she was a factor they were thus far unaware of.

As before, the Winged Man hovered over her, going first. He was uncomfortable and tense in the lobby. His nose wrinkled like he smelled something rotten. In the elevator, he was more relaxed, but he tensed up again as they entered the hallway leading to Monty's apartment. Like before, there was nothing here, but the Winged Man was visibly uncomfortable.

Morrigan tried to hurry up and did relatively well, considering she had to peel the broken pieces of her laptop off of the living room floor. She hoped the hard drive would be intact as she stuffed it in her suitcase, which was still on the floor, magically untouched. She left her toiletries in the bathroom. She had enough from her place. It was time to go.

Because they still had so much time to kill, Morrigan stopped back at the hospital and dropped off a bag of Monty's belongings that she had retrieved from his apartment. He was getting ready for surgery and was out like a light, so they didn't linger. Eventually, they found themselves waiting outside of an electronics store for the door to open at 8. Morrigan was able to get a new laptop and retrieve the information from her broken laptop, thankfully. Then, they were on their way to Doc's.

Chapter 17

Sitting in the waiting room with a still silent Winged Man was awkward for Morrigan. He was contemplative. She was nervous. The secretary said nothing, save for a welcome nicety, but kept looking at Morrigan curiously. Obviously the man sitting beside her was stunning, but it was more than that. Morrigan never so much as spoke on the phone when she was in the office, let alone bring someone with her. It was odd.

Thankfully, the awkward silence didn't last long. Doc was ready for her within five minutes. As she stood to enter his office, Doc holding the door open for her, the Winged Man stood as well. She looked at him quizzically and gestured back toward his seat. He simply shook his head, put his hand in the small of her back and led her toward the doctor's door.

Doc was even more perplexed than the secretary and was about to say something when the man looked at his face. Doc was flabbergasted. He recognized him. As an avid researcher of myths and legends, he would.

"Is your friend joining us, Morrigan?" He asked in the most professional voice he could muster.

"It seems that way, Doc. Sorry, is it okay? It's important that I talk to you, but I -- we" she looked at the Winged Man "-- have a lot going on right now."

"That's your choice, Morrigan."

"Thank you."

The three of them entered the office. Morrigan sat in her usual place and the Winged Man sat beside her, his long frame making the large couch look tiny.

Doc cleared his throat, sat beside them and made a show of shuffling the papers in his lap while he caught his bearings.

"I'm going to let you start, Morrigan. Clearly a lot has been going on and I would like to hear from you."

"I'm just going to blurt a bunch of stuff out for you. None of it is going to make sense, but it is all I can do."

He gestured for her to go on. The Winged Man was staring at her as she spoke, which unnerved the doc. It took all of his training for him to maintain a calm composure. He couldn't be right, but the similarities were so astounding. There was even a whimsical "tint" about the man that suggested something otherworldly or fantastical. He breathed a sigh and waited.

"I'll start with the medicine. Thank you very much. It actually helped a great deal. I slept very well." At this, she blushed and stole a sidelong glance at the man beside her. This confused the doc even more. The man's posture and expression did not change. The Winged Man was unaware that what she was speaking of was their night together. It seemed like world's away to both of them, but was brought to the forefront of her mind when she thought of her drug-laced sleep. The Winged Man was simply too consumed with keeping her safe to even think of it.

"Last night, after I slept, I had another visit from the man who broke into my home. This time, he went to my friend's home, so there is no doubt that he is chasing me."

This time, the man visibly tensed. The Doc missed nothing.

"Was anyone hurt?" He was, of course, concerned, but Morrigan appeared to be in one piece.

"My friend and the attacker." she doubted just how "hurt" her attacker was, but mentioned it anyway. "I plan on leaving until the police find him." Something told her the police would never find him, but it didn't hurt to keep things as normal as possible. "I doubt I will be back soon."

"What about your work, Morrigan?"

He didn't mention her mental health. She seemed composed at the moment, but he didn't want to cause her more fear about what was happening to her. He knew that the stress would not make her anxiety easier.

"I'm giving it to my best line cook, the friend who I was staying with. He earned it and I am finding myself less and less involved with it."

"It's been a few weeks, Morrigan. You're going to walk away from your life's work?"

He was confused. It was natural for her to take a hiatus, but to walk away from her life was an odd reaction. Then again, he thought, there is clearly more to this than meets the eye. He glanced at the unmoving Winged Man as he thought this.

"Yes, I am. I am also moving away. I don't know where yet, but it will be effective this afternoon."

"Will you be in the area for appointments?"

"I really do not think so. This may be our last meeting."

"So I am no longer your doctor?"

"It's kind of sad when you say it that way, but no, you are no longer my doctor."

"Good, then we can do away with the formalities, yes?"

She was perplexed, but agreed. "Um, sure."

"Okay. I recognize the man sitting beside you and am utterly confused."

This caused a reaction, but not the denial he would have expected. The Winged Man looked away from Morrigan and looked at the doc for the first time since walking in the door.

"I suspect I am going to sound crazy, but I have read a lot about him, I think."

Morrigan did not know who he was and the Winged Man didn't want to take the chance of this doctor revealing it, however little the chance was that the doc was right. He spoke for the first time in hours.

"Whatever you think, doctor. I would like it if you kept it to yourself for now." he said in a very polite voice.

"Are you here to hurt her?"

"Does it look like it to you?"

"No, I have to admit that it does not."

"Then how do we proceed?"

"In a different direction, I would think. However, my very *human* curiosity would like to be assuaged. Would I be correct if I said I have seen you before, not in books, but that Morrigan has likely seen more of you?"

"Yes, I saw you when you were thirteen."

It was the year Tynan's father had died. He had nightmares every day for a month. His waking thoughts and sleeping thoughts were very dark. The man sitting across from him had entered his nightmare on the last day. The man was standing on the side of a road, next to his father. His father smiled at the young man and waved. The Winged Man then walked away with his father. After that, he didn't have nightmares about his father anymore.

"I thought so." Doc smiled. "I have the suspicion that I should thank you, but it's just a gut feeling."

"You're welcome." the Winged Man said.

"I thought that too."

There was silence for a moment as Doc absorbed the fact that Morrigan was somehow affiliated with this man in the waking world and wondered if all of his "treatment" of her had been pointless because she was somehow connected to this man. The nightmares, the insomnia, the anxiety. He didn't see how they were linked to the man and doubted he ever would, but knew somehow they were.

Morrigan followed the exchange, which only lasted a few moments. She looked over at the man beside her, which is when Doc realized they were in love. He didn't feel bad that he couldn't help her anymore.

"You know him?" She asked the Winged Man, pointing to Doc. He nodded. "You are going to have to start talking soon, you know." He nodded again. She left it at that.

"I'm not going to keep you any longer, Morrigan." the Doc stood. "It would be pointless to continue this session, considering the, um, circumstances."

The Winged Man stood. Morrigan sat for a second, groaned and then stood. "This is really wacky. At any rate, thanks for all your help, doc. You're the coolest." She surprised all three of them by hugging Dr. Bateson, who stood awkwardly and patted her on the back, his professionalism not leaving him quite that easily.

"Listen, Morrigan. I expect you to contact me as a friend. You have my home number that I gave you for emergencies?"

"Yep."

"Use it." He commanded.

She agreed and left with the Winged Man. Doc stood there shaking his head for a moment and then went to his shelf to pick up a book that had occupied him recently. This time, he turned straight to the page with the picture he had skimmed right past before.

~~~~~~~~~~

Their next stop was a clinical looking lawyer's office across the city. The Winged Man again silently insisted that he follow her into the office and then into her lawyer's inner sanctum. The slightly overweight, young and eager lawyer was a little more rumpled than Doc, but gave in.

Once they were seated, she got to the chase.

"I need papers drawn up immediately for the transfer of Morrigan's and all of its assets to Montgomery Blanchard. He is in my employee records, so you have all of the information you need."

He was taken aback, but figured he would be able to procure a new client and log a few hours out of it, so complied. "I can do that, but immediately is a relative term."

"Today."

"I'll have to put in some hours on this, Morrigan."

"Do it. However, I need one stipulation. I need Monty to give me a payment equal to his former salary for 12 months."

"That is nowhere near the worth of the restaurant." as the lawyer spoke, the Winged Man squeezed her knee and shook his head.

She answered the lawyer first, "It's not in payment for the restaurant. It is so I can survive while I find something else to do." She then looked at the Winged Man.

The lawyer had seen his earlier gesture, so watched the interaction between the two, rather than speaking. The Winged Man shook his head at her again. Morrigan pressed her brows together in a questioning look, willing him to speak. He obliged, but very briefly. "You do not need the money." She decided to wing it and go with it, if it turned out he was wrong or crazy or they both were crazy, Monty would take care of it, contract or not.

"Okay, no money." She addressed the lawyer. "Just give him everything."

The lawyer sighed, maybe he would not be able to do this. "I have to ask you, Morrigan. Are you doing this under duress?"

She laughed. "No, but if it turned out that way, just think of all the lawsuits you could file for me."

He laughed in turn. "All right, I'll get to it. Come back here in two hours. I will need to meet with this Montgomery as well."

"That will not be possible for a few days, at least. I will come back and sign in two hours. I will bring him a copy to sign and he will bring it to you at his leisure."

"Fair enough. See you in a bit."

From the lawyers office, they drove back across town toward the restaurant. Morrigan, sick of the silence, blared an instrumental compilation she had burned months ago for the kitchen, but had never convinced the guys to let her play during a shift. It was metal, rap or nothing in that kitchen. She preferred the metal, but couldn't alienate half of her staff musically.

At the restaurant, Morrigan issued 200 dollar bonuses to each chef and dishwasher, saying it was a thank you for being patient during her absence. She told them about Monty and put her next best chef in charge of the menu in his absence. They all looked at the guy standing next to her with curiosity, but only made vulgar motions at Morrigan when his back was turned to them. She tried not to laugh. They caught on.

Luckily, her front of house manager was on. She delegated back of house ordering, payroll and scheduling to him and told him to delegate receiving to one of the chefs. She retold the story about Monty, but included that the restaurant would be his within days. There was a lot of hugging, swearing to secrecy and farewells involved in that meeting.

Before she left, Morrigan cooked lunch for herself and the man with her. She would miss the kitchen, so she put almost as much love into that meal as she had her first menu at Morrigan's. They ate in silence, but both thoroughly enjoyed the food before them.

It was 1 p.m. before they finished all of Morrigan's chores, but she still had stuff to do for Monty. She wanted to go see him, but had made him promises that had to come first.

She called her landlord and told him she was leaving. He could keep her last month's rent and security deposit. He said he would miss her, which was odd, given that they only met twice, once when her faucet broke and the other time when she signed the rental agreement. After that, she picked up the contract from her lawyer. With that done and a newspaper in her lap, she hunted for apartments for Monty.

Five apartments and no less than 50 digital photos later, she had a few options for Monty. She called a moving company and had them meet her at Monty's. She told them that she would not have a place to move the stuff until the following day, but that she wanted them to pack it up and store it for the night. She insisted that she had already inventoried everything and between her imposing tone and the presence of the Winged Man, she doubted they would steal anything. She was finally ready to go see Monty.

When she came in, he was awake, his leg propped up and heavily bandaged. He was playing games on a game console and apparently getting pissed at them.

He saw her and the Winged Man, who was considerably better dressed after a trip to a department store, and put the controller down, explaining, "My brother stopped by with this damn thing. I should have had him bring me beer instead."

"I think you earned the right to ask for both." She whipped out a manila folder and her digital camera. "I have to go over a few things with you. Do you feel up for it?"

"Yes. Please break the monotony." Monty was not a sit still guy. Even with the meds, he was antsy and needed a cigarette.

"First, you want to look at your apartment options?"

"You took pictures? Christ, you're thorough. I just need a place that doesn't have roaches and does have a place to plug in a microwave."

"You can do better than that. These are all only slightly more expensive than your last place and the chicks will actually stay the night when you bring them over now."

"Bitch." he said jokingly and gestured for him to show her.

One of the apartments had a huge bathroom and tub. The rest of it was nice too, but the obvious selling point was the whirlpool. The man loved sex.

It was awkward for Monty with the Winged Man sitting there all quiet, but he learned to ignore him. Morrigan insisted that she would get him into the apartment with the tub and have his stuff there and a key to the place here before his discharge the next day. He thanked her profusely.

"Don't thank me yet. I am now going to burden you."

He raised an eyebrow and she handed him the manila folder. He read for about five minutes and looked up at her. "Morrigan, this transfers everything to me without any payment agreement. This is not what we talked about."

"I realize that, Monty. Sign it if you want it."

"What the hell are you going to do?"

"Leave for good. I will stay in touch when I can."

"Morrigan, the restaurant is called 'Morrigan's!"

"Change it to Monty's."

"That sounds like shit."

"Montgomery's?"

"Fuck you."

"Just sign it. I sincerely want you to have it."

"I don't want it just because some psycho shit has been going on and you caught a whiff of it."

"That's not why."

"Then why, Morrigan?"

"Because I need to walk away. I built that restaurant from scratch with little help from my partner, who has since fled. I wake up every day, do the same thing, freak myself out at the slightest change and practically live and breathe that restaurant. You take it away and I have a reason to risk doing something else."

"Sentimental speech, kid. Give me a pen."

"That was easier than I thought it would be." she said, handing him a pen.

"I'm greedy, if nothing else."

After goodbyes with promises to keep in touch, Morrigan called her lawyer. He said it would be official when he could meet with Monty. She agreed, left the hospital, then delivered a signed rental agreement to the tub apartment's owner. She delivered the keys and a backpack that suspiciously clinked like bottles bouncing off each other to a sleeping Monty when she was finished and got into the truck with the ever stoic and silent Winged Man. She thought, "This is going to be a long drive to wherever," and pointed the truck toward the highway.

Chapter 18

After nearly two hours of driving west, Morrigan had enough of the truck's radio keeping her company. She didn't mind the Winged Man's staring so much, but his silence was getting on her nerves.

"Why are you not talking? I understand that you may not be conversational, but this is getting ridiculous. With everything that is going on, I haven't received a single explanation from you. Perhaps you do not have one, but it would make sense for us to at least compare notes." she was getting a little worked up. "I mean, why are you here if it is only to hover over me?"

"Slow down, Morrigan."

She looked at the speedometer. She was going more than 90 miles per hour. She eased up on the pedal a little, not willing to let it go at that, though. She waited for a second to see if he intended to say anything else. He apparently didn't.

"No you don't, pal. I asked you direct questions and you are ignoring me. I'm dropping you off at the next exit."

She knew she didn't mean it, but the pained expression that flitted across his face told her that he didn't. He looked glued in place, unable to decide which direction to move, in manner of speaking.

"Okay, I'm not really going to drop you off, but you need to start talking."

"When do you plan on stopping for the night?"

"Probably soon. We need to eat and strategize. Assuming, of course, that you want to help me."

"I do."

"All right, then. Next exit, we find a hotel instead of dropping you off, but I'm reserving it as an option."

Banter was not his strong suit. He just looked at her. She sighed, for once exasperated, but not anxious.

None of the less expensive hotels were to his liking. She would drive up to them, he would wrinkle his nose in distaste and she would go to the next one.

She was starting to feel like a mother with a spoiled child or some approximation of what she assumed they felt like. He wasn't meaning to bother her, but didn't want to sleep -- or, in his case, lie down -- in any of the places with the bad smells. He figured correctly that she couldn't smell them.

They finally rolled up in front of a posh hotel with a Spanish villa motif. He seemed appeased because he jumped out of the truck when Morrigan rolled to a stop in the corresponding parking area.

"Well, this ought to clean us out nicely."

He shook his head. She sighed and walked through the door with him. An overly cheery woman in her mid twenties greeted them at the reception desk.

"Hi. Can I help you?"

"We need a room, please."

She was struck, like everyone, but there is a lot to say about good training in the service industry. She tapped on the keys of her computer for a moment. "Let me see what we have available."

After what looked like mindless tapping for the sake of looking busy to Morrigan, the woman piped up, "Excellent. I have two rooms available. One is a suite."

"We'll take the suite." He said. Smiling at her.

Morrigan groaned. Here we go.

She gave him the price of the room and reached out for payment. The Winged Man simply touched her hand. She got a very dazed look, marked the room as occupied in her computer and dreamily handed them the key.

"Whoa." Morrigan said.

He smiled. "Shh. You'll wake her."

He was right, she was sitting back in her chair sleeping. Morrigan laughed. "I feel bad. What are we going to do about this?"

"She won't remember when she wakes up. I'll convey that the stay was insufficient and we are very upset to the receptionist in the morning. She will comp the room, fall asleep and no one will be the wiser."

"You're going to explain that?"

"I'm going to explain a lot. Let's get settled in. It is time to talk."

They went out to the truck to grab her belongings and those they had purchased for the Winged Man. When they finally got to the room and walked in, Morrigan was getting very excited about the night to come. It might be odd. It might be scary and she might be spending it with a total stranger, or near enough, but she felt safe and excited, nonetheless. She had to admit, he seemed excited too.

The silence reigned again as they walked into the hotel and took the elevator to the second floor. It was a more comfortable silence than before. It was a silence with an end in sight. He opened the door to the room for her while carrying all of their belongings. His strength seemed inexhaustible to Morrigan. Her observations were correct. Here, in the real world, the Winged Man had few limits. Even death would not keep it from coming back the next time he wanted to enter this realm. In reality, one could hardly even call it a body. It was a really good illusion. If he came in true form, it would be different. For example, his demon was real, but still immortal.

The room was amazing. Though Morrigan could have afforded such luxuries at the height of her success with Morrigan's, which was mere weeks behind her, she had never bothered with extraneous space and items. She was simple to the core. However, something about this luxurious hotel suite seemed more suitable for the man with her. Anything less would have seemed like a trash heap with him standing in it. She was happy now that he had chosen this place.

She walked through a sitting and kitchen area to the bedroom. One huge bed. She started getting nervous, but excitedly so. She put down her belongings and went to wash her hands and face. The bathroom was huge with white and gold marble floors and counter tops. The tub, which was situated in the center of the room, was deep and more than large enough to hold four people. It was going to take forever to fill. She began running the water and pouring some of the colorful scented concoctions along the edge into the bath water. A thick aromatic foam began forming immediately. This was going to feel good.

She walked back into the living area and saw the man standing, looking out sliding glass doors onto a balcony and the forest beyond the hotel. His face was contemplative, but as peaceful as she had seen since he came into her real life.

She lightly cleared her throat and he turned to look at her.

"I'm going to take a bath before we get started talking. I'm getting hungry, though and assume you are too. Do you want to call room service?"

He nodded and walked toward the phone. She walked back into the bedroom to lay out clothes for after her bath and grab her toiletries, so she could groom a little before hopping in.

The Winged Man was familiar with the ins and outs of living a normal life here. Having access to the thoughts and feelings of all dreaming creatures helped. However, he didn't know how to guess what Morrigan wanted to eat and he felt it rude to follow her into the bedroom so quickly. He instead ordered one of everything that didn't sound disgusting and added a bottle of wine and two bottles of water.

The surprised service worker on the other end of the phone informed him that his order would be ready in 30 minutes. Twenty-four-hour room service and few guests ordering at this hour was on the Winged Man's side.

He waited while Morrigan brushed her hair and teeth, examined the fading bruises on her flat belly in the mirror and stepped into the bath. When the room service arrived, she had been sitting there for ten minutes and pondering spending an hour in there, slightly draining the tub of cool water and filling it with hot as she went along.

The Winged Man thanked and tipped the room service waiter with money he found in Morrigan's purse on the bed. He figured actually paying a tip was appropriate in this situation. The waiter thanked him and quietly took his leave.

The Winged Man wheeled the cart into the bedroom, sighed and mentally prepared himself for the conversation that would surely be coming soon. He saw that the bathroom door was closed still, but didn't want Morrigan's food to get cold.

Knock, knock, knock.

"Yes?"

Was it him or did she sound nervous?

"Room service is here and may get cold."

"I'll be out in a minute." she said, sounding disappointed.

"Why don't you just cover up a little and I can wheel it in?"

"These bubbles cover everything and that actually sounds fantastic."

He could feel the humidity coming from the bathroom, so removed his flannel shirt and pants, putting on a light pair of shorts they had purchased for sleeping before entering.

She choked back a gasp when she saw the shirtless man wheeling her food into the bathroom. She had seen him naked the night before, but the stress of that night had taken away her ability to admire him properly.

He caught her staring at him and grinned openly. Maybe this wasn't going to be so difficult. Maybe the transition would be easy and he could get her out of this world and with him forever quickly. Probably not tonight, but soon. He relaxed and wheeled the cart toward the side of the tub. Morrigan fidgeted beneath the water.

She looked at the huge spread piled on top of the relatively small cart and laughed. "What did you do?"

"I wasn't sure what you wanted, plus, I am hungry too, so I will eat what you do not. It really wasn't a big menu. It just looks like a lot because you are expecting less."

She laughed. "All right, tell me what you have."

"I have a Greek salad, Cobb salad and garden salad. From there, I have mushroom ravioli . . . "

"I love mushroom ravioli, so I am sure I will choose that, but I will take the Greek salad first."

"Don't you want to hear the dessert menu?"

"Not yet." she said through a wide grin.

He handed her the salad and a fork then started to walk away.

"Wait." she said without thinking first. When he turned, she was stumped for a moment, but quickly recovered. "Don't you want to eat too?"

"I can wait until you are done. Just let me know when you are dressed and I will come back in and get my food."

"Don't be ridiculous. This tub is big enough for more than the two of us. You could get in and eat without ever touching me."

He stared blankly and she lost her confidence.

"That is, if you don't mind sharing a bath with me." she mumbled.

He didn't. He politely removed his shorts, leaving on the boxers underneath because he didn't want to freak her out, then stepped into the bath. She was relieved that he had not found her invitation odd or had rejected her. Ever since he got here, she had this odd fear of rejection, this protectiveness and a myriad of other feelings overwhelming her in his presence.

They both laughed the moment he was in the water and awkwardly seated across the tub with his knees drawn, so as not to touch her.

"Your food." they spoke at the same time.

"Close your eyes."

He was a little taken aback by the request. He rarely closed his eyes . . . ever. She had expected an immediate response because he had been so polite and so did not wait for him to comply before turning to set her food on the marble edge of the tub, standing up and reaching for a starter dish from the cart. Her head turned from him, she asked if he wanted to start with a salad. He thickly replied "Yes," not knowing what else to say.

He stared at her naked body, slim, slightly bruised, but stunningly beautiful. Just in time, he realized why she had told him to close his eyes and closed them to save her the embarrassment of seeing this strange, tall man starting at her.

The water made a delicate splash as she sank back into it.

"Okay, open."

He complied immediately this time, longing to set eyes on her as soon as possible.

"Here." she handed him a salad.

They ate their salads in a silence full of words to come, then began their main courses. In the middle of the main course, the water began to chill and she did her trick of draining some cool water and adding some hot. The lower water level revealed his hard stomach because he was so tall. It barely revealed the upper part of her breasts, despite her own height. She did her share of staring before she realized he was watching her.

Embarrassed and unwilling to ruin the moment by being awkward and leading to the end of the best bath of her life, she looked away, waited for the tub to refill and finished her dinner quietly. By the end of the meal, the water had gone cold again. It was time to get out.

He was done with the charade and ready to move on to the important business between the two of them. He stood up, having discarded his boxers in the middle of the meal. She was speechless again, red-faced and unsure how to proceed. He pulled the plug on the tub, slightly unfairly leaving her with no other option than to sit there and have her nudity revealed or to stand and get over this shyness. He retrieved two towels from a nearby cabinet and stood next to the bathtub with one, spread open, waiting for her to step into it.

He himself was dripping wet, but he thought it more important to nurture their trust in each other than to dry himself off.

She stepped, frightened, but willingly into the towel. He wrapped it around her body and began rubbing her skin dry. All of sudden, she felt as she did in her nightmares, safe, secure, loved, halfway to total abandon. She leaned against him as he hands worked at drying her skin. When she was nearly dry, she gently escaped his embrace and grabbed the second towel from him. Silently and diligently, she dried his skin, reaching far up to get his muscular neck and shoulders.

Dry, they walked out of the still warm bathroom into the bedroom. Without having to say it was time, they dressed in their pajamas, the Winged Man retrieving his shorts from the bathroom and Morrigan picking the only pair of sweats she had that she hadn't been wearing with holes in them that dated back to her college years.

They wheeled the cart out to the living area, both knowing they would be sitting and talking for quite some time. Morrigan left the wine on the cart, grabbed a bottle of water and curled up on the couch with a soft throw that was resting on it. The Winged Man sat next to her, but pulled his feet off the floor and faced her with his legs out in front of him. He reached for her and they wound up lying down with Morrigan between his legs and her head resting on his chest. He stroked her hair for a moment and then lifted her chin so she was looking up at him.

"I know you have been waiting for me to explain some things and I apologize that it has taken so much time. Some arrangements took precedence and required your full attention. This also requires your full attention, so I thought it best to wait until we were free from other commitments and potential dangers to you."

"Apology accepted." she moved so she was sitting up facing him, as she wanted to be able to comfortably look at him while they talked.

"I have a long story to tell you and you may not believe some of it."

She interrupted.

"Do you mind if I ask some of my more pressing questions first and then we can fill in the details?"

"Whatever you want, Morrigan."

"First, what is your name? It's embarrassing, but I have thought of you as "the Winged Man" for a long time."

The Winged Man? So, she had made the connection between him and her nightmares, he thought.

"I don't really have a name, but I understand that is a little . . . odd. You can call me whatever you want."

"I will call you the Winged Man, then, pending nicknames." she blushed, realizing she had just implied that she thought they would become very familiar with each other.

He waited patiently for the next question.

"I'm going to come out and ask something you might find hard to believe and hope it isn't too weird, but, have we met before yesterday?"

"Yes."

"How often?"

"Quite often. Since you were a little girl, in fact."

"So you are the man from my dreams."

"Man from your dreams?" he laughed and she cringed, but he put a hand over hers and squeezed to show that he was not laughing at her. "They are more like nightmares, Morrigan. You have never strayed to dreams, that I know of."

"How do you know that?"

"That is part of the long story, Morrigan. Do you want me to begin?"

"Not yet."

"Okay." he waited patiently again.

"Am I going crazy?" the question took some nerve. She didn't really want to know.

"I do not think so. The events that make you wonder that are very real, though you may not believe me and go with the "crazy" scenario anyway." he hoped not. That would complicate things and he would have to spend a lot of time convincing her to of her own sanity.

"Do you recall all of the events in my nightmares?"

"Yes, probably more than you do."

"So, last night, before you showed up at Monty's?"

He smiled. "Yes, I remember that very clearly."

She almost cried. "Everything about you there, they way you treat me, the things we do, our . . . feelings are the same for you here as there?"

"Very much."

"We're in love?"

"I know that I love you."

In a rush of words, she told him how her only reality had ever been there with him. She told him how much she always looked forward to seeing him, how hard it had been to think he was not real and that the life she had to live would never be enough to replace the world she thought she was making up in her mind. She nearly cried, but instead hugged him fiercely and kissed him for the first time here, in this dreary world. Everything lit up. The dull edges of her near constant anxiety melted. The unreal quality of the world fled. She had found that which anchored her. She had realized her connection to this being, whatever he was. It was the single most important and relieving moment of her life. She was safe, she would be safe, she would be happy. Euphoria never felt so good.

The Winged Man gripped her upper arms with his hands.

"If you continue doing that, our conversation will have to put off and it is important."

She felt like a child who was ignoring her lessons.

"Sorry."

"Don't be. Do you have any more pressing questions?"

"I think you are about to answer all of them."

"I think so too."

This time, she lay with her head on his chest and just listened.

He told her a bit about his realm, the pockets of dreams and nightmares and how he and is brothers had spent all of mankind's existence manipulating them, creating them and walking in them. He explained that that was how her doctor knew him, though he kept the personal details of Tynan's dream out of it and did not mention the mythology of man regarding he and his brothers.

He told her about how he found her among the nightmares, a little girl, unafraid and possibly even a puppet master of his creations. He told her that she was unique and it had taken him a long time to find out how. He told her how, when she became a woman, his feelings about her had evolved, but also how he had waited years to find out exactly what could be between the two of them before he admitted that he loved her. He told her how he had been afraid of her mortal life and how inaccessible she would have been to him if she had died. He told her how he had not been able to watch her constantly, but that he had others doing so. Some of his kind, but not quite like him, each with different powers, with different jobs.

Morrigan was starting to piece together what he was talking about. A land of gods. This is where he lived. He was a god or something like one. This was understandably difficult to swallow for her, but she had seen enough and was completely convinced of the veracity of his statements, given the detail with which he described their forays in her childhood up until now. As he had predicted, he mentioned some things she did not remember.

Throughout his talk, he left out the Fiend -- something he would regret later. They talked a little about Eric and both apologized for their stupidity. He, for letting her get hurt, she for not being more careful. He is appalled by her apology, but leaves it at that because he has to explain Eric stalking her now without bringing the Fiend into the picture.

"Eric was deeply disturbed when he died. When he came back, he was still disturbed and you were the last effort of his life. His last game, so to speak. He was stuck in it, still craving victory. That is why he follows you. He won't hurt you now, though."

He had told the truth and she didn't press for details. She trusted him. This made him feel bad, but there was nothing he could do right now. She would know everything if he could get her from here. He hoped it might be tomorrow, but could not gauge where she stood at the moment.

He revealed that the light and dark sides of himself were represented by the man she always saw and the demon she first saw glimpses of after he killed Eric. He explained that he was neither primarily good nor primarily bad, but that perhaps good was relative and the two of them were suited anyway. She agreed. Finally, he asked the question that was weighing on his mind.

"Can you accept this, Morrigan?"

"I believe I already have, but really, I just have to see what tomorrow brings and the next day."

He could handle that.

"Okay, so we're done telling stories, I think."

It had taken them hours to go over every detail that he cared to convey.

"Yes, I think so too."

"Are you tired?"

"Not yet, but I may want to sleep before I get on the road." That gave her pause. "Wait, what happens if I fall asleep?"

"I will meet you there."

"Oh. Good."

It gave him pleasure for her to want to be around him as much as he wanted to be around her. He lifted her up by the elbows, so she lay on his body with her face in front of his and her feet far above his. Their lips touched again with the same result as before. Touching him, being intimate with him, being near him, grounded Morrigan. Deep below the erotic sensations that overwhelmed the surface, something was clicking into place. This something, if ever torn asunder, would destroy her. She felt it, but was intensely distracted.

His bare chest rubbed against her t-shirt and she longed to have it off. As was quickly becoming his habit, he simply ripped it off her body with one effortless movement. His long-fingered hands moved down her back and slipped into her pants so they gripped her bare bottom. He spread her legs by pulling apart the very tops of her thighs with his strong hands. From behind, the fingers of his right hand found their way to the slick fluid and soft skin he was seeking. He absentmindedly rubbed the warm liquid seeping out of her onto her thighs and buttocks, quickly darting slightly inside of her and back out to continue rubbing. He loved the way her skin felt with his hands sliding all over it. He wanted to cover her in oil and rub his body on her for hours. He imagined it as he thrust his pelvis toward her legs so she could feel his hardness through her thin sweatpants.

She bit at his lip gently and darted her tongue out to lick the same spot. She ran her hands over his shoulders, chest and neck helplessly. She wanted to feel all of him all at once. She could not keep her hands still. His fingers flirting in and out of her and only occasionally, very briefly, sliding up and down her was teasing her in the sweetest, most desperate way.

Her hands finally sought something to grab onto. She moved her right hand down into his shorts and let her fingertips just graze the length of his hardness. He gasped and thrust his penis toward her hand. She thought of the sensations caused by his teasing fingers, now pressing gently, but constantly. Then, one finger left its place and dipped ever so slightly inside of her. Another flicked at the spot that was making her so crazy. She groaned. No, he wasn't getting the immediate pleasure he sought.

Her other hand reached down the front of her own pants. She sought the area where his hand was resting and played with his hand for a moment, gathering some of the moisture that had him so fixated. He moaned and pushed her hand out of the way.

She moved her other hand away from his penis and he gave a sound reserved for those who have pleasure taken away from them suddenly. Her other hand quickly took its place. Morrigan slowly ran the slick moisture on her fingers down the length of his shaft. Another intimate, helpless sound escaped him. He thrust and thrust, but all she would give him was a very gentle pressure, made smooth by her own wetness.

His oily fantasy and fascination with her wetness was not enough to sustain him any longer. At least, not with his fingers. He moved himself out from underneath her, very rapidly and left her facing down. She gave a surprised squeak and felt momentary disappointment and the lack of warmth on her fingers and lack of fingers on her warmth, but she was soon overcome.

He straddled her from behind, with one knee on either side of her thighs. He yanked her sweatpants down just below her ass to the top of her thigh and then lay on top of her. He thrust his cock down in the space between the top of her thighs. It was so slippery that the length of it slid all the way down into the warmth with no coaxing. A sound of pleasure escaped his lips. He used his hand to press it against her in all the right places and began to move it up and down the length of her.

In mere moments, she was seeping onto the blanket below her. He reveled in her obvious pleasure, kissing her neck, telling her how much he loved her, how beautiful she was, how sweet she felt to him. All the while, he was holding back his own pleasure in order to maximize hers. The steady rhythmic pressure had Morrigan ready to burst when he stopped suddenly. He lifted her by wrapping his arm around to the front of her waist and scooping his hand over her wetness. He carried her this way to the bedroom, where he lay her gently on her back.

He kissed her softly on the lips and undressed her completely. He kissed her nipples, her stomach and gently spread her legs. He put his face between her legs and used his tongue to lick the sweetness off her. His tongue flicked and pressed as he watched her face soften in pleasure. Finally, she grabbed his hair and her pleasure poured onto his waiting tongue.

Barely a moment after the shivering in her legs stopped, he stuck one long finger inside of her and sucked at the tender spot above it. She gasped and arched her back. His finger moved inside of her, pressing against something she never felt before. He loved the way it made her move, made her entire body blush, but he stopped. That would be another day. He lifted himself over her and slid inside her. He was so large, he could hardly push into her. He did so gently, watching for signs of pain, but all she did was kiss his face, his eyes, his shoulders while doing her best to move her hips against him. He let go inside of her with a feeling of wonder. She was his, in this world and his. They would stay together from now on. That is what he thought and there was nothing to warn him otherwise.

Chapter 19

They are together, again, in the ballroom. Morrigan feels fierce and strong. She is wearing a deep black dress that he had made onto her body, showing her how he builds these nightmares. He is trying to show her how to manipulate them more or, at least, willingly, but she is having a hard time being confident enough. Her confidence peaks when he throws a nest of what looks like living razor wire at her. She transforms it, without thinking, into a nest of snakes in mid air. They hit her with a meaty, harmless thunk and slither off her onto the floor, scattering toward the armor and disappearing inside.

"Now do it on purpose."

She stands there, concentrating on the armor, trying to move it, do anything to it, but nothing happens. She looks at him, still feeling her own strength, but becoming exasperated. Just looking at him makes her want to take him right here. She wants to tangle herself in him, make him want her so badly that he never stops to bother with these silly exercises. As she thinks about seducing him, her clothing transforms until she is wearing a thin black gauze from head to toe. Her entire body is visible beneath it. It is as if she stands in a thin black mist, naked, muscles flexing. He groans.

"Knock it off, Morrigan. I'm getting distracted."

"I'm sorry. I just can't do it on purpose."

He looks pointedly at her body and she glances down.

"Oh. Well, it looks like I can."

She imagines herself naked against him and him powerless to refuse her. Now she is really naked. She laughs triumphantly, but also finds the fun in doing this and so, instead of acting on her initial wish, she erects a barrier of black fluid between them. She presses her body against it so her shape shows through on his side. Just as he reaches for her, the fluid falls in on her, enveloping her until she wears something like a moving, flowing, black latex from neck to toe.

"That is no less alluring, you know." He winks.

She steps toward him.

"Oh, I know." she says, as she runs her hand down his chest and disappears. She reappears on the salt throne seconds later.

"I like sitting here."

"You should. I made it for you on your 18th birthday. It contains all of the nightmares of those whose nightmares you invaded and walked in before I made you a series of your own."

"You told me about that, but not about this chair."

"It was a gift that I could not give you. You never felt fear here, but you always felt sympathy for those dreaming that you stumbled across who feared the nightmares their minds suggested to me. So, I trapped them here so they would not have those fears again."

"Aren't you supposed to scare them, though?" She is remembering the glittering salt and the suffering within. The pictures had looked familiar to her then, but she had not noticed the feeling of familiarity. Now she does.

"Not quite. I create a place for their mind to be when they are sleeping. They decide whether it will be a nightmare or a dream. They do not make the decision consciously, but their conscious mind decides what occupies it and I give it infinite possibilities. If you're afraid of your toaster, I give you a toaster that eats you alive. If you are consumed with thoughts of your lover, I give you dreams that exceed true love."

"Narcissist." she says through a laugh.

"Oh, no. I've never become that lost in anything."

The way he said it was funny to her, as if he took the word very literally. He did. He knew that story very well.

"We're about to wake up and you are making progress. You ready to go?"

She would have hated waking up a month ago, but she is more than ready to now.

They woke up in a large cottage on an island. The Winged Man had procured it for them through his questionable means, but he promised her that the kindly landlord would have money in his bank account, but that the Winged Man just wouldn't be handing it to him personally, as the landlord thought he was. She didn't question it.

~~~~~~~~~~

Morrigan's eyes opened up to the Winged Man's human face hovering over her. He kissed her on the nose.

"We need food, Morri. Do you want to come with me?"

"Yep."

She got out of bed refreshed. She had been sleeping better than she had in her entire life this past month. They both slipped into comfortable clothing, hugged and peeked in the refrigerator.

"Crap."

"You've been hungry. I should have went yesterday."

"I'm hungry now. *I* should have went yesterday."

He scooped her up and carried her out to the truck.

"Let's get you fed." He said, as he stuffed her into the truck.

As they drove to the dock, the Winged Man was wrapped up in thoughts both happy and tormented. He had something to tell her, something that would change his plans drastically, something that she would find out soon enough. He decided to tell her on the boat. He could then take her out for breakfast and then take her shopping. She needed to eat soon.

They both donned the jackets they kept in the truck for water crossings and sat comfortably in the boat. They loved it out here. They were both content, but he knew that he could only be content here for so long. He had yet to check in on the Artist, but was sure the other was checking in on him. He had work to do, but didn't want to live without Morrigan. This was getting complicated.

"You're pregnant."

She looked up at him, confused, as if he had spoken another language.

"I can tell. I can . . . see the baby. You are pregnant, Morrigan."

"What are you talking about? I ..." she thought about it and realized that it had been nearly two months since she had her period.

"That's possible?"

"Oh, quite."

"You knew it was possible."

He sighed.

"Yes, but I was optimistic. I figured we would be gone from here by now." she looked at him apologetically. She had wanted to get the hang of being "there" while knowing it was really real. She had asked for time.

"I'm glad we stayed." he quickly added.

"But, you wouldn't consider this. . . " she pointed to her stomach ". . . a good thing?'

"Well, it's wonderful, in its own way."

"I . . . I had never even thought about having children, but I suppose it is sort of wonderful." she said matter of factly.

"There is a catch, Morrigan."

She sighed and lifted her face to the sun.

"I don't know what will happen if we leave here while you are pregnant."

"What do you mean?"

"I don't even know if you will stay pregnant."

"Then we will have to wait eight months. I'm sorry." she kissed him on the nose "I know you want to get home badly. You can always go and come back for me."

"It is an option, but it also has a catch."

"Of course it does." she was starting to get nervous. She was getting a little sweaty and the hunger in her stomach fled so nausea could take its place.

"The baby might not be like you."

"Of course it will, I am its . . ." her words caught in her throat. Their conversation about her being so unique played in her mind, her heart sped up and her mouth dried. She was going to vomit.

He threw his arm around her shoulder and rubbed her back as she retched over the side of the boat. It stopped quickly and a painful knot lodged in her stomach.

"There has to be something, Morrigan. I do not want to be without you."

"I . . ." she realized something monumental. "I don't want to be without either of you."

He had known it would come down to this. He wanted the child too - desperately, but what would they do? There was no way he could be both there and here for the duration of the child's life, hoping, perversely, that Morrigan would outlive it so he would still be able to take her with him.

"We'll find a way, Morri."

The boat drifted. The two of them were silent, both filled with different thoughts. Morrigan, thinking of having to be separated from him, the Winged Man thinking about the Fiend and his deals . . .

Chapter 20

Morrigan and the Winged Man spent four perfect months on their island, both planning and plotting in their own ways. The Winged Man was contemplating how to bring the child with them and if it would be necessary to leave the baby they had both come to love here. They could watch it grow and visit it often, but he wasn't even sure Morrigan would be able to visit.

It was all unknown to him. Soon, he would have to leave her and seek the advice of those who knew better than he what would become of Morrigan and the child. He didn't want to leave her, but he could wait no longer. There were a few months before the child would come and, if it had to stay, he had to find it a good home. He would also have to selfishly convince Morrigan to be with him rather than their child. He hated himself for it, because he knew he would have a relationship with the child outside of its dreams, but what of her?

While the Winged Man tortured himself with thoughts of loss and love, Morrigan thought only of love. She was oblivious to the sacrifice she may have to make. She imagined the Winged Man and herself laughing with a small, black-haired and blue-eyed angel. She even wondered if it would have wings. Her visions were complete love.

The two of them sat in the bath, both contemplating the lovely rise in her stomach when he decided to broach the topic of him leaving for the time being.

"Morrigan, I have to go back for awhile to sort some things out before the baby is born."

He anticipated her precise answer.

"Why not handle it while we sleep? I have been sleeping so much better. There should be plenty of time."

"When we are sleeping, there are limits to where we can go."

She understood. "You're not going where I can go."

"I'm not sure. It may be as simple as going home, but it might be much more."

"How long will you be gone?"

"It could be a few hours, love. It might be a few days as well, but no longer than that."

She sighed. He could see that she hated the idea of separation as much as he did, but she did not question him.

"Okay. When will you leave?"

"Well, now that we have established that I am leaving, I will probably leave tonight. It makes no sense to wait any longer."

She snuggled against him, wordlessly giving her consent.

~~~~~~~~~~

That night, before he left, they enjoyed sweet moments, her completely given over to the bliss she had found, he on the verge of panic. When he left, telling her not to leave the island for anything, he almost came back immediately. Nothing seemed important enough for this, but then he imagined the same child that consumed Morrigan's thoughts. There was no choice. He had to go.

He sought out his brother first, finding him in a birch wood, stylized tree house of sorts. They greeted each other and the Winged Man asked the question he came to ask.

"It's relatively assured that she can come over, but I recall something a long time ago. A set of twins, in fact. One took on the qualities of the father, one the mother. In other words, only one was capable of transition. It could be nothing more than a story, but it sounds right to me."

This had not settled the Winged Man's fears. His torment was clear in his eyes, but his brother went on.

"You may have a better chance, given that Morrigan is . . . special and you are even more so, but I would be prepared for any outcome, brother."

"Is there any one who would know more about this?"

"Not that I can think of. Father's memory obviously goes back further than ours, but you know there has been much less of that sort of 'activity' for hundreds of years. They have a way of forgetting what isn't recorded for them too, you know. If there were something written, I would know it."

The Winged Man knew this to be true. His brother had read everything on his kind, written by both mortals and immortals. There was no one else to ask.

"You know, brother, I have been watching you and thinking."

The Winged Man nodded for him to go on.

"There is no reason for this sort of adoption you are mulling over. It is possible for us to take turns. Not the Fiend, of course, but you and I."

One eyebrow on the Winged Man's face shot up.

"Are you talking about establishing a rotation?"

"That is exactly what I mean. Unfortunately, if the child cannot come here, it would last a mere lifetime or as long as the child wanted us with him or her. I can't see it being too much of a problem. It would be over . . . "

At this, he rested his hand on his brother's forearm.

". . . in the blink of an eye for us."

The Winged Man did not resent his brother's plainness of speaking. It was what he needed.

"Yes, no need to even clear it, really."

"Precisely. So, it is decided. How long do we wait to see if the child can come?"

"I think we will go to the three immediately after the birth. There is no sense waiting. Morrigan will last forever with us here, but she will not there. I can't stand being there with her any longer than necessary."

"I will go straight to them when the time comes. You stay with Morrigan."

"Thank you."

He paused and then voiced another concern that had been weighing over his head these past months that he had been "training" with Morrigan and avoiding talking to his brother.

"The Fiend. Has he returned?"

"No. He has not. I think he is not in a certain someone's good graces."

"At least he did the right thing."

"Can we even be sure of that?'

"Why would he be given refuge there after his usefulness was up?"

"Maybe it isn't."

Realization sparked in both of their eyes. It was not the look of two men who had just discovered something essential that pleased them. It was the look of two men, who, if given their way, would scorch the world and the universe beyond. Neither said a word. The Winged Man disappeared on the spot. The Artist became a blur headed toward the blackness beyond their realm. His only thought as he traveled was relief that the Winged Man was not with him as he heard a tortured scream shake the blackness of the underworld. It was then that he realized what deal had been struck.

Chapter 21

Morrigan is dancing with her child in the ballroom, his eyes the only color in the room, the rest a blackness that joys him.

She knows, in her sleeping state, that this can come to be. Her child will come with her. There is no doubt that her baby is both like her and like his father. He is here, with her now, in his own way. As she dances, her arms wrap around the soft warmth of her child. Her only wish is that his father were here with them.

Out of the darkness, a spear is launched at them from the wall of armor. She turns swiftly, unable to protect her child and affect the change needed to stop it simultaneously. The spear enters at the base of her spine and she awakens to a brief explosion of pain.

~~~~~~~~~~

Panting in the darkness behind her, she could hear the sloppy, half-dead squelching of the Eric thing's decomposing corpse. She bravely turned her head to face him and found that was the only part of her body that she could move. She saw him, his right arm somehow inside her, pulling her from the back. Around his arm was a black liquid. She screamed as she realized it was her blood.

Morrigan died as he pulled her spine free through her skin. Her last thought was of her baby and how her nightmare, created by her, was wrong. Her scream was not one of pain, but one of loss. It was the one the Fiend and the Artist heard as she entered the realm of the dead, her dying scream still issuing forth. The former listened, completely content with his handiwork. The latter was mortified.

The Winged Man entered the room at the moment of Morrigan's death. She did not see him there, nor did the Eric thing. He was made aware soon enough, as the demon burst forth from the Winged Man and he tore the beast off her, managing to pin it to the ground with one massive leg, as he stood over his dead lover, sobbing and apologizing in a language that certain sects of humans would recognize as that of their greatest foe. At last, when the pain had made the permanent impact that allows us to move on, he seized the dead Eric in powerful arms and said, "I will see her again. All you will see is torment."

They landed on the terrace before the gates. Like the Fiend before him, Eric was chained by the Winged Man. The demon within him created a cocoon of living, moving web around Eric and was satisfied to hear the creature's pain as the web moved around him, burning him, stabbing and cutting him, while keeping him alive. It could stay that way forever, if the Winged Man so wished it and, at this moment, he did.

Epilogue

The Winged Man appears in the realm of the dark man. He finds his brother and forces the Fiend to bring him to Morrigan. They find her on the shores of the river, writhing in pain, though there is nothing there. Her back heals and is torn apart repeatedly before his eyes. He reaches to grab her and free her from the deal his brother made. As he touches her, he simultaneously sees the child, still alive in the way things live here, inside of Morrigan, and hears a voice behind him.

"As you have forever banished me from your realm, so you are banished from mine." says the dark man.

Before he can get a hold on Morrigan, he is forced back to his corner of this world. He rushes at the barrier repeatedly, but can't get through. As he loses his mind, one brother stands by his side crying while the other stands outside of his line of view in the darkness, laughing.

Made in the USA
Lexington, KY
21 July 2012